A Puss in Boots Retelling

The Marquise

AND

Her Cat

SHARI L. TAPSCOTT

FAIRY TALE KINGDOMS
BOOK ONE

ALSO BY SHARI L. TAPSCOTT

Silver & Orchids

Moss Forest Orchid

Greybrow Serpent

Wildwood Larkwing

Lily of the Desert

Fire & Feathers: Novelette Prequel to Moss Forest Orchid

Eldentimber Series

Pippa of Lauramore

Anwen of Primewood

Seirsha of Errinton

Rosie of Triblue

Audette of Brookraven

Elodie of the Sea

Grace of Vernow: An Eldentimber Novelette

Fairy Tale Kingdoms

The Marquise and Her Cat: A Puss in Boots Retelling

The Queen of Gold and Straw: A Rumpelstiltskin Retelling

CONTEMPORARY FICTION

The Glitter and Sparkle Series

Glitter and Sparkle

Shine and Shimmer

Sugar and Spice

If the Summer Lasted Forever

Just the Essentials

The Marquise and Her Cat: A Puss in Boots Retelling
Fairy Tale Kingdoms, Book 1
Copyright © 2017 by Shari L. Tapscott
ISBN: 9781986540582
Editing by Patrick Hodges and Z.A. Sunday
Cover Design by Shari L. Tapscott

For Grandma
I think you would have liked this cat.

CHAPTER 1

Etta

THE CAT STARES AT ME FROM HIS PERCH ON THE WINDOWSILL. His fluffy, golden tail twitches back and forth like a pendulum, and I squirm under his gaze. Even when I look away, his green eyes never leave me.

Sunlight shines through slits in the closed shutters, and dust motes dance in the air. It's daytime; he should be in the mill, catching mice. But, as if he knows Mildred's dying, he waits with us.

Before my eccentric aunt fell ill, she would talk to the cat —have real conversations with him. She'd even answer like he was actually speaking to her. It was the strangest thing. Disconcerting and unnatural.

My brothers, Thomas and Eugene, sit at the table with their hats clutched in their hands as we wait. The village doctor has been in Mildred's room all afternoon. When we woke this morning and found her barely breathing, we didn't expect her to make it past noon. It's nearing evening now.

The tiny cottage is too still. I'd like to open the shutters and let in the warm spring air, but the darkness feels right for the occasion.

Needing something to distract me from the cat's intense stare, I pick up my darning from the basket next to my chair. Eugene, the eldest of us, ripped his best shirt last week. Unlike the old brown rag he wears now, this one hasn't needed mending yet. Now it will match all the rest of ours.

My dress has so many patches, it looks like a quilt. With each of my growth spurts, I've added another layer to the hem and occasionally let out the waistline. At seventeen, I think I've finished growing. Maybe after the harvest we'll finally have enough money for me to buy material for a new one—if Mildred leaves the mill to us, that is. If she doesn't, I don't know what we'll do.

Mildred's door opens, and we all turn. The silence is palpable. The doctor nods. His expression is solemn, remorseful. I let out a held breath.

It's over.

Our aunt was a strange woman, and though I lived with her for ten years, I never knew her well. She kept to herself mostly, tending her garden and letting the boys run the mill. The only company she kept was that cat.

I glance at him now, morbidly curious to see if he will somehow sense her passing. Perhaps he'll mourn her loss— maybe he'll recognize the gloom weighing on my shoulders and wish to comfort me as well.

As I watch, the cat stretches. After arching his back and bowing low as if stiff from his morning in the sill, he stands on his hind legs and lifts the window latch with his nose. Without so much as a backward glance, he presses the shutters open and jumps outside.

He's a very odd cat indeed.

"TO EUGENE, MILDRED HAS LEFT THE MILL AND COTTAGE," the ancient village clerk tells us.

My brothers and I sit in front of the man's desk, pretending our entire livelihood doesn't depend on what he's going to tell us. When he says the words, we all visibly relax. Though we hadn't discussed it out loud, each of us worried Mildred had sold the deed back to the baron at some point in the last few years.

The man owns most of the village, and his rent goes up every summer. With the meager amount our mill brings in, there's no way we could afford to stay.

The clerk continues, "And to Thomas, she has left the donkey."

I sigh, sitting back in my chair. There's nothing else. Should my eldest brother decide to take a wife, which he likely will if Sarah-Anne, the butcher's daughter he's been courting, has a say in the matter, there will be nowhere for me to go.

"To Suzette…"

I suck in a breath, surprised, and sit up straighter. What else did my aunt own?

"Mildred has left her cat."

From the corner of my eye, I see Eugene and Thomas share a startled look.

"I beg your pardon?" I ask, sitting unnaturally still.

The *cat*? That's just an insult.

The clerk frowns at the paper and adjusts his frames. He shakes his head and then pulls a tiny, jingling coin pouch from his desk drawer.

My heart leaps. There might not be much there, but it's at least something.

"And this"—he holds the money between us—"goes to Master Puss."

This time, I look at my brothers. "Who is Master Puss?"

The clerk clears his throat. "I believe it's the cat, Etta. And it says here that the money is to be used to buy him a pair of boots."

A lump forms in my throat. "Boots...for a cat?"

Looking uncomfortable, the clerk gives me a sympathetic nod.

I blink several times as I accept the pouch. Truly, Mildred was mad.

The clerk goes over a few more legalities with my brothers, but I'm too consumed with humiliation to listen. My aunt, my own flesh and blood, left the last of her earthly savings to a barn cat—for a pair of boots, no less. Boots for a cat when I haven't had a new dress since I was thirteen.

I rise when my brothers stand, dip when the clerk gives me a respectful nod, and follow Eugene and Thomas out the door. We startle a goose, who must have decided the entry was a good spot for her afternoon perch sometime while we were inside, and she squawks as she waddles several paces away, flapping her wings with indignation.

Oh, goose, I feel your pain.

Around us, the village bustles with activity. It's a market day, and farmers from the outskirts have hauled in their early spring crops. There are stalls with spinach, radishes, and all kinds of lettuce. The tailor's young son and daughter have even set up their own makeshift stall and are selling asparagus that they must have picked near the large creek that runs outside of town.

The vegetable grows with profusion this time of year. I can't see a reason to pay for it when I can gather it myself, but there are people more benevolent than I am. Or, rather, people with money to waste. How I'd love to have a few coppers in my apron pocket to give to the girl and boy. I'm sure they're hoping to make enough to visit the new chocolatier who's just opened his shop in the main square.

It's very fancy—a little too fancy for our quaint village, truth be told.

Still, I hope the young man does well. He wears finely-tailored coats and has a hat to match each pair of boots he owns. Though I would never admit it to Eugene or Thomas, I like to look at him. Like to imagine that someday he might look back.

"Etta, where's your mind?" Thomas laughs like I've done something humorous.

I jerk my head toward him. "What?"

He's a year older than I am, a year younger than Eugene, and he's as ornery as the donkey he inherited. And right now, he's grinning at me. "You just stepped in goose droppings."

I groan as I pull my skirt aside so I can examine the slipper. Disgusting greenish goo is smeared along the thin leather bottom. With one foot in the air, I stumble and then hop backward a few times to regain my balance.

Eugene's eyes go wide, and he holds out a hand. "Suzette—"

The warning is too late. I've already backed right into someone. I leap forward and whirl around. "I'm so sorry…"

The words die on my lips, and I gulp. At first horrifying glance, I mistakenly think it's the young man from the chocolate shop, and I freeze in mortification.

But, no. This man is a stranger. His hair is corn silk blond, and his eyes are blue. But like the chocolatier, he wears a fine coat with well-cut breeches, and his boots are made of expensive leather. Along with a dagger, a rapier hangs from his baldric and rests at his hip.

With the way he's dressed, he must be a lord's son at the very least, perhaps even the offspring of a duke or an earl.

And, right now, his eyes are laughing at me.

My face flames, and for one brief moment I consider darting down the street to hide.

The young man bows. "Good day, mademoiselle."

Let me die right here on the street.

I dip in a curtsy and lower my eyes to the cobblestones as I mumble, "To you as well, monsieur."

I'm extremely conscious of my skirt with all its patches and my goose-dropping-smeared slipper. Never has such a fine man addressed me. Not once, not ever.

"Perhaps you can help me," he says. "I'm looking for the bookshop."

"It's just around the corner," Eugene offers, obviously embarrassed for me—or possibly of me. "The first building on the right."

The man looks at Eugene and nods his thanks, and then, just as he's about to step away, he hesitates. Turning to me, he says, "Do you think you could show me?"

"Me?" I blurt out before I can think better of it.

Eugene cringes and Thomas, trying to keep himself from laughing, bites his bottom lip so hard it turns white.

"Yes...yes, I'd love...of course," I stutter, feeling like even more of a fool than I did before.

Giving me a polite, refined sort of smile, the man offers me his arm. Practically trembling, I accept. He nods to my brothers, wishes them a good day, and leads me away.

CHAPTER 2

Beau

I STAND AT THE TAILOR'S WINDOW, ARMS AT MY BACK, AND look across the cobblestone street. Without turning, I ask, "Who's the girl?"

The tailor, a man of middle years with a mess of red hair, lifts his lenses, glances up from the table he's working at, and squints out the window. "Do you mean Etta?"

"The one standing there with the three men." Two of them wear the simple clothing that most of the men of the village favor. They belong. One of them, with his fine doublet and self-important, puffed-up noble appearance, does not. The man looks vaguely familiar, but since I've only been in Glenridge for a season, I can't place him.

Anderson nods and looks back at his project. "Yes, that's Etta. She lives in the mill."

"Where is that?" I ask absently.

The dress she wears, a strange thing that looks like it's been mended and lengthened a dozen times, doesn't do a thing for her. But the moment she smiled at that man, instantly besotted with him, her cheeks turned pink, and something caught in my chest. Now, inconveniently, I can't

7

seem to take my eyes off her, off her bright eyes and the rich, light brown tendrils of hair that have escaped her bun.

And now I'm waxing poetic like a fop.

"Just outside town, not far from the road to Rynvale," Anderson answers. "The two to her right are her brothers, Eugene and Thomas. Their aunt just passed. I'm sure they're sorting the will out." He looks up, his face set in a somewhat pinched expression. "If Broussard doesn't already own everything."

Monsieur Broussard. Not the most pleasant man I've ever met. The widower baron lives on a hill just outside the village, his estate positioned to overlook everything he owns, which is a good portion of Glenridge. With no interest in living as a tenant, I bought my newly-opened shop from him outright. He certainly charged me enough for it—not that it hurt me any. It doesn't matter, anyway. I'll make my money back when I leave. That's a skill I learned well enough from my father.

"An odd woman, their aunt," Anderson continues, and then he grimaces. "May she rest in peace."

I frown instead of asking about the peculiar nature of the woman because the third man, the pompous one, offers the girl his arm. She flushes an even brighter red, tucks her hand at his side, and walks off with him with stars in her eyes and a smile on her lips, completely oblivious to Anderson's dog, who's just leaped from the stoop and is barking like a mad thing. I watch them until they turn the corner.

Only once she's gone do I pull my gaze from the street. Vaguely disconcerted, I turn away from the window.

CHAPTER 3

Etta

"I'm Kerrick," the man says after a few quiet moments.

My eyes are trained on the street in front of me. A sheep has gotten loose from a farmer's pen, and a boy of about eleven tries to chase it back to the market stalls. The tailor's dog, who moments ago was napping in the shade of a tree, now runs after the pair and yaps with canine glee.

Trying to look casual, I glance at my companion. Does he know he looks so very out of place here?

"Suzette," I answer, though very few people call me by my given name.

"Do you live in Glenridge, Suzette?" he asks. "Or are you here for market?"

I swoon a little when he says my full name in that cultured way of his. His voice is just perfect—medium in deepness and smooth.

"I live on the outskirts of the village." I hesitate. "In the cottage beside the mill."

I hope he's not familiar with it. It's rundown and shabby, and our own field hasn't done well in years. If it weren't for local farmers needing us to grind their wheat, we'd practically be beggars. Unfortunately, in the last few years, many have built their own small mills and no longer need ours.

"And what brings you to Glenridge?" I ask, pretending that I stroll with members of the nobility every day.

"The man who runs your bookshop is said to have a variety of rare fiction. My father's birthday is next week, and I'm hoping to find him something he doesn't already have."

Judging from Kerrick's clothing, I imagine that's a difficult task.

"He likes to read?" I ask, and then I feel foolish.

Of course the man must like to read. Why else would Kerrick be looking to buy him a book?

"He's fond of stories of adventure." He waits a beat. "As am I."

I finally work up the courage to glance at the man at my side. He's impossibly handsome, his face almost cherubic in its beauty. If I were to guess, I would say he's only a year or two older than I.

We reach the bookstore in less than a minute. I pause outside the door and motion him toward the sign. "Here you are."

He turns and looks at me—really looks at me—and then he smiles. "I'm happy to have met you, Suzette."

An idiotic grin toys at my lips, but I manage to give him what I hope is a demure smile. "And I you."

With one last nod, he turns into the shop.

My stomach can't decide if it's light with butterflies or churning with another sudden bout of melancholy. The short walk was easily the most exciting thing that's ever happened to me. Now it's over, and I'm sure nothing this wonderful will ever happen again. I'm the orphan niece of the newly-deceased miller's widow, and the only belongings I have in the world are a cat and enough gold to buy him a pair of boots. Even I'm not enough of a daydreamer to pretend I'll see the man again.

With a sigh, I walk down the street. The cobbler's sign hangs just three buildings down. I might as well get it over with. He's going to laugh at me. Who has ever heard of a cat with a pair of boots? How is the mangy creature supposed to wear them?

He'll most likely yowl his fool head off when I try to pin him down long enough to slip them over his paws.

I'm standing outside the entry, staring at the sign, when the cobbler opens the door.

"Etta?" he asks, surprised to see me on his step. "Can I help you?"

I draw the pouch of coins from my satchel, glance at my threadbare, stained slippers, and make a hasty decision. "I'd like to buy myself a pair of boots."

CHAPTER 4

THE BOOTS ARE STURDY AND MADE OF SUMPTUOUSLY SOFT, supple leather. They are the most extravagant thing I've ever owned, and I've hidden them in the back of my corner of the loft where my brothers won't find them. It's been a month, and yet every time I look at them, I'm consumed with guilt.

My dying aunt had one final request, and I was too selfish to honor it. Not only that, but the money could have been used for something more practical—like food or repairs to the mill.

This morning, my brothers are planting the field, and I'm inside, scrubbing the dredges of the last week of pottage out of the old cast-iron pot. Every night, we eat a little of the grain-based porridge, and every morning, we toss in a few vegetables. Sometimes we add a few scraps of meat if we have them (and we rarely do). But I've had enough today. It's time to start fresh.

The cat—my cat—watches me from his favorite spot in the sill. I've opened the shutters, and the sunshine streams down on his tawny brown fur.

"Shouldn't you be catching mice?" I ask. As I say the words, I begin to wonder if I've gone as mad as Mildred.

Of course he doesn't answer. His only response is the slow twitch of his furry tail.

"Do you miss her?" I say again, simply because I have no one else to talk to. "Are you lonely?"

I dump the hot water outside the window, place the newly-cleaned pot over the fireplace, and brush away a long strand of hair that hangs in my face. Not looking at the cat as I speak idly to him, I go about my morning business. When my chores are finished, I pull a basket from its hook by the door and step into the sunshine.

Immediately, the cat rises from his perch and trots out with me. When I turn to close the door, he stops as well. I give him a sideways look and continue toward the patch of forest just beyond the field. I wave to Thomas and Eugene when I pass them. They fight with the donkey, who, as usual, has decided he doesn't want to cooperate. It doesn't matter whether it's the cart or the plow we attach to him, the beast never wants to earn his keep.

Eugene calls after I've passed, "Where are you headed?"

I swing the basket forward. "I'm going to look for mushrooms."

My eldest brother nods and goes back to his chore. I frown at him. He owns the mill now. Why hasn't he asked Sarah-Anne yet? Surely she's growing impatient.

But I know the answer. It's because of me and Thomas. If Eugene marries, where will we go? What will we do? Thomas could take a job as an apprentice, but what about me? I very much doubt Sarah-Anne would want me to stay. Even though Eugene has moved into Mildred's room, there's still very little privacy in the tiny house.

The day is too beautiful to dwell on such thoughts, and I push them out of my mind.

To my surprise, the cat follows me into the forest. He trots at my side, pausing every once in a while to pounce on insects in the weeds.

This part of the woods is perfect for hunting for the marnelle mushrooms that grow in the spring. They like warm, sunny hillsides, and they often pop up near fallen trees. Since it rained yesterday, there's a good chance I'll find some before I have to turn back.

Before I start foraging, I walk for a while, breathing in the scents of spring and seeing if I can catch a glimpse of the sprites that are rumored to live in these trees. It's peaceful, quiet except for the leaves rustling in the bare breeze.

I find my first mushroom in a sunny patch near a decomposing tree. After checking it over, careful to make sure it's safe to eat, I pop it in my mouth and close my eyes. It's hard to believe something so lowly can taste so decadent. The winter was long, and I'm so sick of pottage.

After I've walked for a mile or more, I sit on a large boulder to the side of the path. I glance at my slippers and frown when I see the leather has worn through near the ball of my left foot.

"What am I going to do about that?" I ask the cat, since there is no one else around.

"Why don't you wear my boots?" he replies. "With as large as you had them made, they certainly won't fit me."

Startled, I scream and leap to my feet. My basket goes flying across the trail, bounces off of a tree trunk, and falls to the ground. The mushrooms I've harvested scatter.

I back up until my shoulder blades press against a cool shelf of rock. With nowhere else to escape, I look about me, frantic.

"Thomas?" I call out, my voice shaky.

Of course it was only my brother playing tricks on me. I'm not sure how he slipped away from Eugene, but it's just

14

like him. Growing irritated, I lean forward and look for him. Now that he's heard me talking to the cat, he'll tease me about it for the rest of the foreseeable future.

Slowly, I turn my gaze back to the cat. He sits on the boulder I just vacated, and, as usual, he's watching me. I eye him, wary.

Thomas doesn't know about my boots.

"Cats don't talk," I say, feeling the need to remind myself out loud.

His whiskers twitch. "Not usually."

I scream again, push away from the rock, and race down the path. In my haste, I trip over an exposed tree root and crash to the ground. Ignoring the pain, I attempt to scramble to my feet, but I'm not quick enough. From behind, the cat leaps on my back and lands in front of me.

In what looks like feigned dignity, he sits on his haunches and begins to groom his face. "You should be more careful. You've ripped your dress again. Weren't you just complaining about that the other day?"

I clench my eyes shut, refusing to look at him. I can't seem to draw in a full lungful of air. Whatever Mildred had was catching. I've contracted her sickness, and now I'm suffering from her same hallucinations. Panic tightens my chest, and my throat thickens.

No...it was the mushroom. It must have been a poisonous one after all.

Somewhere in the back of my mind, a little voice tells me I've collected them since I was tiny. I know what the safe mushrooms look like, and the one I ate was edible.

But it's either the mushroom was poisonous or my cat can speak.

Eyes still shut, I say out loud, "It's because of all this festering guilt—that's why I've imagined this. I have to tell Eugene and Thomas about the boots."

"You don't honestly think you're—"

"No!" I hiss, opening my eyes again. "You can't talk!"

Tilting his head, looking more amused than a feline should, he closes his mouth.

"Cats don't talk," I say again, making sure he understands.

As if he's mocking me, he mews.

With a near hysterical laugh, I shove myself up and examine my ripped sleeve. Sighing, I rub my eyes and glance around. Everything looks just as it should. If I'm hallucinating, shouldn't things look…off? Blurry perhaps?

I walk back to retrieve my basket. I pick up one of the fallen mushrooms and study it. It's just like the ones we've eaten every spring. After tossing it back to the ground, I peer at the cat.

He's followed me, staying right with me like before. Frowning, I leave the rest of the mushrooms where they lie, pick up my basket, and head back to the cottage.

AT SUPPER, I CONFESS MY SELFISH PURCHASE TO MY brothers.

"Why would you do that?" Eugene asks, more confused than angry. "I would have thought you would have rather bought material for a new dress."

I bury my head in my hands. "I don't know. When I saw the cobbler on the cat's behalf, it was all too ridiculous. I'm so sorry I wasted the money."

Thomas laughs. "I'd rather you own a new pair of boots than that cat."

Eugene nods and scoops a spoonful of pottage into his mouth. It's boring tonight—plain mushy grain and nothing else. It would have been better with mushrooms at the very least.

"Hiding them in the loft doesn't solve anything," Eugene says. "You bought them; you should wear them."

I let out a slow breath. This didn't go as badly as I had imagined, and yet, I still feel guilty. But hopefully the conversation will clear my conscience, and I'll no longer have episodes with talking cats.

After our meager supper, I climb the ladder to the loft. Years ago, when we first moved in with Mildred after our parents died, we separated the boys' side from mine with a large, shabby blanket. It doesn't offer much privacy, but it's nice to have a small area that feels like it actually belongs to me.

The cat sleeps on my pallet, and when he hears me, he stretches, yawns wide, and then promptly goes back to sleep.

I'm being ridiculous. The cat didn't actually speak.

Trying to ignore him, I pull my boots from their hiding spot. I glance over my shoulder, half-expecting something from the cat. He doesn't pay me any attention.

Shaking my head, I sit and stroke the soft leather. I'll wear them tomorrow.

I set them on the floor and change into my night clothes. Careful not to disturb the cat, I slip between my blankets. After the day I've had, I'm sure sleep will never come, but then, before I know it, it's morning.

With a yawn, I stretch. When I look at my feet to see if the cat is still there, I find him gone. In the light of a new day, the idea that he actually spoke to me is simply absurd. Of course I imagined the whole thing. It was lingering stress and guilt from losing Mildred, that's all.

As I'm plaiting my hair, the cat jumps up the ladder to the loft. He sits, watching me.

"I'm sorry I was harsh with you yesterday," I say quietly, hoping Thomas is already up and gone. "I don't know what's wrong with me."

He tilts his head and saunters to my boots. He knocks one over, falls to his side, and grasps it in his claws like it's a plaything. I watch him for a moment, somewhat amused. When he pokes his head in it, almost getting himself stuck, I take it away.

I peek around the hanging room separator, making sure Thomas is truly gone, and then settle onto my pallet. Pulling the cat onto my lap, I stroke behind his ears. He breaks out into loud purrs, and I bury my head in his fur.

"What am I going to do?" I ask him, holding him close. "Where am I going to go? No one will marry me. I don't even have a chicken for a dowry."

He pulls away and gives me a haughty look.

I scratch his back. "Don't look at me like that. It's not my fault no one wants a cat."

Again, he nestles close to me. I pet him for several more moments, and then I sigh.

"You won't mind if I wear your boots, will you?" I feel ridiculous asking him.

The cat yawns. I'll take that as a no.

"That's very kind of you." I pull the boots on and let out a long, contented sigh. "All right. Let's get our chores done."

CHAPTER 5

Beau

THE DOOR OPENS, AND I LOOK UP FROM THE ROASTED COCOA beans I'm shelling, hoping, as I always do, that this new patron will be the one I'm waiting for.

Apparently, it's not my day.

Two giggling girls, daughters of one of the wealthier farmers, step into the shop. I try not to groan and, instead, don a smile. "Good afternoon, Louise," I say, nodding to the eldest and then the next. "Maria."

They attempt to hold back laughter while they bat their eyelashes shamefully. I'm a novelty here, the son of a wealthy lord with connections in the far tropical islands of the southern seas. A new face, a new story. Unattached and unspoken for. And, unfortunately for the girls in Glenridge, not the slightest bit interested in these sweet young country bumpkins. Except one. But she's not here.

She hasn't even paused outside my door.

Nevertheless, being a man of business, I lean on the counter and give the girls a friendly smile. "What can I do for you today?"

Louise smiles brightly, as if I've addressed her alone, and glances at her younger sister. "Maria, mother wants you to help with the laundry this afternoon. Go on now, I'll be right behind you."

Maria opens her mouth, and her eyes narrow in irritation.

I'm about to intervene before the feathers start flying, perhaps offer them a free sample of chocolate, when I see the girl I've been watching for, Etta, pass by the front windows.

"Excuse me," I say to the sisters and leave them gaping as I hurry out the front.

She's gone by the time I push through the door. I stare down the street, contemplating which way she went. I see her constantly now, but I haven't had the right opportunity to introduce myself.

A soft touch on my shoulder draws my attention back to the shop.

"Monsieur Marchand?" Louise asks. "Are you quite all right?"

I look down the street for several more moments before I nod and usher the pair inside. "Yes...I'm sorry. Now, what can I help you with?"

It takes several minutes for the girls to make up their minds and even longer to scoot their reluctant selves out the door. When they finally leave, I find myself staring into the street, thinking of the girl I've yet to speak with, wondering about her. I twist the signet ring on my finger, reminding myself I have a purpose for being here—and it has nothing to do with chasing after the miller's sister.

From across the street, the baker's daughter waves to me. "Good afternoon, Monsieur Marchand!"

With a sigh that I smother with a smile, I wave back. As I step into my shop to finish shelling the cocoa beans I've neglected, I shake my head. This is ridiculous. I have a chocolate shop to establish, an ogre to find, and I already have more than enough female distraction.

The last thing I need is to let myself become besotted over a girl I've never even met.

CHAPTER 6

SPRING TURNS INTO SUMMER. THE DAYS GROW LONG AND WARM, and the wheat grows tall. For the first time in over two years, we may have a decent harvest come late summer. The forest is thick with greens and berries, and Mildred's tiny vegetable garden is flourishing with all the rain we've had lately.

With little to do today, Thomas is at a neighboring farm, helping build fences. He's smitten with the farmer's daughter, and he's been there almost more than he's been here. Eugene chops wood in the shade of a large tree, and I shell the last batch of spring peas on the front steps. It's peaceful, blissfully hot, and all I want to do is nap—not that there's any time for that sort of thing.

My cat spent the morning hunting mice, but now he's lounging in the sunshine at my feet.

"I can't keep calling you Cat," I say.

I've taken to talking to him again. Even if he's silent, he's better company than most.

He sits up, his green eyes trained on me.

"Well?" I ask. "We'll have to come up with something."

I toss another empty pod in the pile I'll take to the compost later.

"How about Bartholomew?" I raise my eyebrows when he wrinkles his nose. "Too long? What about something short, like George?" His tail twitches, and I smile. "Fine. Then why don't you just tell me your name?"

"I don't think you'd like that very much," he says.

I freeze, my eyes on the pot of peas. Slowly, I raise my gaze to him. Glancing at Eugene to make sure he's out of earshot, I whisper, "Cat...did you just speak?"

He wiggles his whiskers. "We're making great progress, you and I. You're not screaming and running down the road as if I have the plague."

My stomach tightens with unease. Deep down, I've known since that day in the woods no matter how I tried to tell myself differently. In fact, it's possible I've just been waiting for him to finally make himself known.

"Why did you never speak to me before?" I ask, going back to my task like it's nothing to have a conversation with one's barn cat.

"I didn't feel like it."

I raise my eyebrows. Of course. He is a cat, after all.

"So tell me, why do you feel like it now?"

He stands and stretches, the movement long and slow, and extends one leg and then the next. "I was born for grander things than this mill. You're going to help me attain my destiny."

I laugh. "You were the runty kitten from the butcher's litter. You're not destined for grander things any more than I am."

Sniffing the empty pods I've already shelled, he says, "You're meant for grander things as well." He looks at me. "And my name is not 'Cat,' it's Master Puss."

"Oh yes, I do recall that. It's a bit high and mighty, don't you think, Feline?"

If a cat could roll his eyes, his would right now.

"I'll call you Puss," I say as I scoop him into my arms and scratch behind his ear. "I simply will not refer to you as 'Master' anything."

He struggles to get away, but then, unable to take it any longer, begins to purr. "Very well. Now let me go. We have things to do."

I set him aside. "We do?"

"I'm going to teach you to hunt."

I LIE FLAT ON MY STOMACH AND STARE AT AN EMPTY MEADOW not far from the mill. The sun sinks low, and soon I'll have to return home to prepare supper.

"What are we doing, exactly?" I ask Puss.

"*We* are not doing anything. *I* am going to catch a rabbit. You are going to watch." He crouches low, and his hind end twitches in anticipation.

"Then why am I on the ground?"

"So you don't scare them off. Now stop talking."

I'm about to say something else anyway, but suddenly the cat lunges forward. A rabbit darts out from the cover of a bush, but he's not fast enough. Puss leaps on his back, rolls with the creature in his clutches, and the rabbit goes limp.

The cat sits and turns my way. I assume this means he wants me to come now. Obedient, I push myself to my feet and make my way toward him. The rabbit lies still on the ground, perfectly unblemished.

"How did you kill him?" I ask, surprised.

Puss licks his paw, obviously pleased with himself. "I snapped his neck."

"Impressive." I gingerly pick the animal up by its paw. "We'll be eating well tonight."

"There will be more for that later. This one goes to the village."

"Why?"

Already trotting toward Glenridge, Puss says, "You're going to trade it for a bag."

I hurry to keep up with him. "A bag? What kind of bag?"

Tired of questions, the cat hurries ahead, ignoring me until we reach Glenridge. "Go see the tailor. Hurry before he closes shop."

With a frown, I hold the poor creature away from me as I walk down the street.

A few people I know call their greetings, and several people give me odd looks. It's not every day I carry a dead rabbit through the streets.

I'm almost to the tailor's when the young man from the chocolate shop turns the corner. Our eyes meet, and his gaze drops to the rabbit. For a fraction of a moment, I mistake him for the man I escorted to the bookshop. My heart picks up its pace, and I nearly drop Puss's kill.

But the chocolatier's hair is short and brown, not blond. It's not light, nor is it dark, but a perfectly normal, unremarkable color somewhere in between. There's a handsomeness to him, even if it's not in a conventional way. Most of his features are plain, but for some reason, he's striking— even if nothing in particular truly stands out.

I can't help but notice he's immaculate, as always, and here I am in a dress covered in dirt. With my free hand, I quickly brush strands that have escaped from my braid away from my face.

He smiles. "Your pet has seen better days."

"Oh," I glance at the dead creature I'm holding, and my face grows warm. "It's not–"

"I didn't figure it was. You do have a purpose though, don't you?" His eyebrows furrow, and he motions to the rabbit, a secret smile in his eyes. "Or do you simply make a habit of walking the streets with a dead hare?"

"I'm going to the tailor's." My cheeks grow almost painfully hot, and I can feel the blush spreading to my neck and ears as well. "To trade the rabbit for a bag, if he'll have it."

"What kind of bag?" The chocolatier takes a step nearer, and his smile grows.

I gaze at him for several moments, off-kilter. As he grows closer, I notice his eyes, which I assumed were brown, are actually green like the smooth, pale rocks I would sometimes find at the bottom of the creek when I was a child. It's an unusual color, unsettling but fully mesmerizing.

"I don't really know," I finally answer.

He gives me a quizzical look and appears to be fighting back an amused grin. "I have a bag, but I have no rabbit. Perhaps we could make a trade?"

A laugh builds in my chest. Before it can escape, I mentally slap myself. "Yes…of course. If you would like the rabbit, that would be fine."

With a nod of his head, he motions for me to follow him to the chocolate shop. As we walk down the street, I glance back at Puss, who is sitting on a fence post at the edge of town. His tail twitches, and I can feel waves of feline judgment roll off of him.

I wrinkle my nose at the cat and then transfer all my attention to the man I'm walking with.

"I'm Suzette," I say after a moment.

He turns. "Really? I was told you preferred Etta."

"You've asked about me?" Though only curious, my voice sounds a little high-pitched, like maybe his answer means more to me than it does.

Looking faintly embarrassed, he clasps his hands behind

his back and looks forward. "You come to the village several times a week, and yet you've never visited my shop."

It's my turn to look uncomfortable. After all this time, I still come to Glenridge hoping to run into Kerrick at the bookshop. Of course I haven't seen him. After all, how many birthdays can his father have?

Idly brushing more dirt from my dress, I say, "I'm afraid your shop is a bit extravagant for my family's budget."

"You didn't hear?" he asks.

I dare a peek at him. "Hear what?"

A slow smile builds over his face, making him look even more handsome. "I offer free chocolate for every customer who comes to trade a rabbit for a bag."

Laughing out loud, I say, "You do not."

He nods with earnest. "Yes, I do." His smile twitches to crooked, and he laughs. "I implemented the incentive just moments ago."

"I've told you my name. What's yours?" I ask softly. The question is forward, but I don't care.

His smile softens, and his eyes grow warm. "Beau."

I give him a small curtsy, which is awkward with the rabbit in my hand. "It's a pleasure."

He unlocks the shop door and motions me inside. "Truly, Suzette, the pleasure is mine."

The smell is indescribable. The moment it hits my nose, I stop and close my eyes. The fragrance is sweet and rich. It's nothing short of decadent.

"It tastes better than it smells," Beau assures me.

"Impossible." I take another deep breath and then open my eyes.

"Shall I relieve you of the...?" He motions to the rabbit, still amused.

"Yes, please." Just as he's taking it, I pull it back, teasing. "As long as you have my bag."

"I do." He grins. "I swear."

"Very well." I hand the rabbit over, more than happy to be free of it.

After promising he'll be right back, Beau climbs the stairs to his living quarters. As I wait for him to return, I browse the confections behind the counter. They're all tiny. Some are covered in icing like cakes, but others are simply brown.

"They're all too pretty to eat," I say when Beau comes back down.

He goes behind the counter, chooses several of the small candies, and wraps them up.

"You really don't have to—"

Beau hands me the package, cutting me off. "These are for later. I have something else I want you to try now."

Almost as an afterthought, he hands me a satchel-sized bag with a drawstring top. It's nicer than anything the tailor would have traded me for.

"Thank you," I murmur.

I glance around the shop. The windows are fitted with glass, and various pieces of art hang on the walls. My gaze, again, drops to my dress. I don't belong here.

Beau takes out a small pot and adds milk and a chunk of dark brown chocolate to it. "Every morning, I roast the cocoa beans in a large pot over the fire. Then I shell them and grind them with sugar until the hot mixture is a thick, buttery liquid. After that, I let the concoction cool in blocks." He places the milk and chocolate mixture on a grate over the low-burning fire. "That's how I make chocolate."

I take a seat on a stool and cross my arms on the thick wood counter. "Where do your beans come from?"

He stirs the milk with a wooden spoon, and the chocolate slowly melts, turning the white liquid brown. "From tropical regions far over the seas. A traveling merchant who has a route to Rynvale delivers them to me once a month."

"Have you ever been there, where the cocoa beans grow?"

Beau removes the steaming liquid from the grate and then pours it into two porcelain cups. "I have. My father captained a ship, and I traveled the world with him before I set out on my own."

I notice the way he stumbles when he mentions his father in a past-tense way. How long ago did he lose him? Since we've only just met, it would be very rude to ask.

"And yet you find yourself here," I say instead.

"This was my father's land. After he passed, I felt as if it was my duty to visit." He slides a cup to me.

I breathe in the steam. "You almost make it sound as if you're not here to stay."

He leans down across from me, resting his elbows on either side of his cup. "Who's to say? Will I make my home here forever?" He shakes his head. "Not likely. But I'm here now."

Feeling warm, I take a small sip of the drink in front of me and suck in a gasp. The mixture is dark and sweet— sweeter than honey and richer than the coffee I had forever ago on a birthday long passed.

"What do you think?" Beau asks.

"It's the most delicious thing I've ever tasted." I take another sip. "Thank you."

He drinks from his own cup. "It's becoming quite popular with the nobility."

"Why did you choose to set up shop in tiny Glenridge? You'd have likely done better in Rynvale, near the castle."

"I like it here, and we're close enough to Rynvale. The elite can come to me if they wish."

Somehow I make the drink last far longer than it should, and it's dusk when I step out the door. My brothers will be missing me.

"Thank you for the bag," I say.

Beau holds the door. "Thank you for the rabbit."

A warm, friendly moment passes between us. Just as I'm wondering if it's foolish holding hope of seeing Kerrick again when this man lives right here in the village, a loud and insistent yowl sounds behind me.

Closing my eyes and gritting my teeth, I say, "That would be my cat."

Beau peers around me into the street. Puss sits in the middle, an unamused look on his feline face.

"He's handsome, isn't he?"

Puss *is* handsome—brown and large with long, luxurious fur, but he's also a nuisance—was before I even knew he could speak.

"Thank you again," I say.

Beau's eyes are bright in the dim light. "Come back and see me."

I bite back a smile as I nod and turn away. Before I can go, he catches my hand and draws me back. "Promise me."

My chest grows warm. "I promise."

CHAPTER 7

"Stop sniffing around the boy at the chocolate shop," Puss says. "I have greater things planned for you."

We're nearing the mill, and it's grown dark. The summer moon is just cresting the horizon, and crickets chirp in the underbrush.

"He's the son of a captain, cat," I say, coming to Beau's defense even if I don't believe I was "sniffing around" Beau in the way Puss means. "And he's very fine."

Puss only makes a disdainful snort—a practiced sound only a feline could execute well.

"I still have to wonder if I'm going mad," I say. "I can't grow used to you speaking."

"You'll have to accustom yourself to it. I don't plan on stopping now."

The cottage's shutters are open to the night, and cozy light glows from within. I prepare myself before I go in. Eugene will likely lecture me for staying out so late.

When I walk through the door, I'm greeted by a feminine laugh.

The scene before me is so domestic, I hesitate in the door frame.

"Hello, Etta," Sarah-Anne says from the fire.

She wears a long apron over a pretty dress, a dress I've never seen before, so it must be new, and she dabs butter over a browning hen on the spit. Eugene is at the table, watching her with that wistful expression he gets whenever she's near, but Thomas has eyes only for the bird.

"Where did the hen come from?" I ask as I hang my new bag on a hook by the door.

It's been a long time since we've had this much meat. Sometimes we barter for eggs, and Thomas will occasionally bring home fish on the days Eugene doesn't need extra help with the field or the mill, but chickens are a rare treat. They have been since we lost our laying hens to a fox who sneaked into the hen house last summer.

We still haven't been able to replace them.

"I did some extra mending for Mrs. Fletcher. In exchange, she gave me the bird," Sarah-Anne says.

"It was kind of you to share."

I pull my precious package of chocolate from my apron. Tonight I have something to contribute as well.

Sarah-Anne waves a hand likes it's nothing. "We have too much as it is."

Uncomfortable, I look out the darkened window. It must be nice being the butcher's daughter.

Sarah-Anne notices the looks on our faces. Instantly paling, she murmurs, "I'm sorry."

Eugene goes to her side. "Don't be sorry. The field is growing well this year. By autumn, we will have recovered."

The blond-haired girl smiles up at my eldest brother, and they share a look that makes me feel as if Thomas and I are intruding. Again, a pang of guilt plagues me. I have no doubt the two would be married already if it weren't for us.

Thomas, obviously thinking the same thing, busies himself with his knife and a short, thick limb that he's whittling.

"What are you making this time?" I ask from behind him as I look over his shoulder.

My brother works with agile fingers. "I'm not sure yet."

"I think it looks like a fairy."

He glances back at me. "You always think they look like fairies in the beginning."

I shrug and look for something to occupy myself with. Sarah-Anne seems to have supper taken care of.

"Why were you out so late?" Eugene finally asks.

Grimacing, I take a seat next to Thomas. "I met the chocolatier. He invited me in."

The room goes quiet, and every eye turns on me. My brothers don't say anything. They're obviously a little shocked that the man would speak with me.

"Be careful with that one," Sarah-Anne says, her voice quiet.

I turn to her, ready to defend Beau. "He's kind."

She gives me a small smile. "Yes, and a little too handsome, perhaps."

"What does that mean?" I ask.

Sarah-Anne wrinkles her nose. "Everyone's quite taken with him, but he seems a bit aloof." She pauses. "A little high and mighty, if you will."

Her words don't match the man I met. Beau is friendly and generous…and the way he looked at me made me feel special. I've never felt special before.

Except for the time I accompanied Kerrick to the bookshop.

I bite my lip, thinking again of the young man I haven't seen since the beginning of spring. How did he infiltrate my thoughts so completely? It's been months, and yet I can still

33

remember his smile after an encounter that lasted only minutes.

Eugene watches me with narrowed eyes. "You've grown rather pretty, haven't you, Etta?"

Offended, I frown at him. "Are you saying, at some point, I was a troll?"

My older brother laughs, but he looks uncomfortable. "I've never stopped to notice, is all. Perhaps you should be careful."

Heat stains my cheeks, and I look away.

Changing the subject, Sarah-Anne goes on to tell us about her day, but I barely listen.

Though I'm sure they're wrong about Beau, he's not the man in danger of breaking my heart.

THE SUN IS NEARING ITS APEX IN THE SKY, AND I'M, AGAIN, lying on my stomach, flat on the ground. Sharp weeds stab at me, and meadow grass tickles the bare skin on my arms. Like before, we're just beyond the mill, still on Eugene's land.

"Now, as soon as the rabbit wanders in the bag to eat the greens and grain," Puss instructs, "you're going to yank on the string and trap him inside."

A young, fat hare sniffs around the edges of the bag. I wait, wondering if this will truly work. Then, before my eyes, the foolish creature hops into the bag. I yank on the strings and successfully trap the rabbit inside.

"It worked!" I exclaim as I leap to my feet.

"It won't work again if you don't keep your voice down," Puss hisses. "You'll scare away everything within a mile of here."

My stomach sinks when I see the poor rabbit struggling against the confines of the bag. "Now what—"

Before I can say the words, the cat leaps onto the bag, catching it in his clutches. Within moments, the rabbit goes still. Horrified, I stare at the lifeless bundle.

"Next time, you'll take care of it," Puss says. I begin to shake my head, ill at the thought of snapping a living creature's neck, but the cat hisses. "I can't do everything for you."

Gulping, I nod.

Two and a half long hours later, I've bagged four rabbits. Covered in dirt and feeling weary, I carry the full bag into Glenridge.

"Take them to the butcher," Puss says, and then he narrows his bright green eyes. "Not the chocolatier."

I roll my eyes and stalk down the street. I push through the door to the butcher's shop. Sarah-Anne sits behind the counter, plucking a chicken.

"Etta." She smiles when she sees me. "What can I do for you?"

Her father steps from the back when he hears he has a customer.

I set my bag on the counter between us. "I have three young rabbits that I would like to sell."

Surprised, Sarah-Anne raises her eyebrows, but the butcher only opens the bag. He inspects my catch and nods.

"These are fine hares, Etta. You don't want to sell the fourth?"

"Thank you, sir. And no, that's for our supper."

After he weighs them, he hands me five copper coins. "Tell your brothers I'll buy more if they trap them."

"Oh, I..." I shrug. What difference does it make? "All right."

Sarah-Anne gives me a wave as I slip out the door, and I walk into the street, very satisfied to have coins jingling in my apron pocket. I find Puss on his favorite fencepost at the edge of the village.

"Now go to the tailor's," the cat says, "and buy a pair of breeches and the material to make yourself a shirt."

"Breeches?" I ask him in disbelief.

Puss twitches his whiskers. "You can't hunt in a dress. Go."

Giving in, I turn back toward the tailor's shop. And then I wonder why, exactly, I am taking orders from a cat. But the answer is simple. I have more coins in my pocket than I've ever earned on my own. And they're mine.

The tailor's dog naps on the stoop, and I give him a quick scratch before I step into the shop. I find the tailor's wife, Patricia, sitting in the corner, stitching together the bodice of a gown.

"Good afternoon, Etta," she says as I close the door behind me. "What can I help you with?"

"I need a pair of breeches." I pause as I look over the bolts of fabric on the wall. "And some muslin."

Patricia sets her work on the chair. "For Eugene or Thomas?"

I rub my cheek. "For me, actually."

Her eyebrows shoot up, but she goes into the back and brings out a simple pair of breeches in a dark color not unlike Beau's blocks of chocolate. "I suppose these will fit you."

"Thank you." I examine them, wondering how strange it will feel to wear trousers after a lifetime spent in a skirt.

She gives me a funny look, one questioning whether I've parted ways with my modesty, but she only nods.

After I pay her, I leave the shop with my new breeches and the fabric for my shirt. Only one copper coin remains in my apron pocket. I hold my purchase close, pride blooming in my chest that, for the first time, I bought something with money I earned myself.

"Now what, cat?" I ask when I reach him again.

"Now we go home. You have a shirt to sew."

And a garden to tend, berries to pick, laundry to wash, bread to bake, and supper to make. I heft my bag over my shoulder. At least we'll eat well tonight.

When I reach the mill, I find Thomas working in the vegetable garden, doing the weeding I promised I would tend this morning.

I toss my bag at him. "I'll finish in the garden if you dress this for me."

He looks in the bag. Astonished, he asks, "Where did you get the rabbit?"

"I caught it."

I'm not sure Thomas believes me, but he carries the bag to an old stump in the shade of a tree. Before I start on the garden, I take my new breeches and fabric to the loft and leave them on my pallet.

In the evening, I stew the rabbit.

"Meat two nights in a row," Eugene says as he finishes off his plate, looking pleasantly full. "Imagine that."

Warm with pride in my contribution, I toss Puss another generous helping of scraps before I climb up the loft to start on my shirt. The cat soon follows, and I work by candlelight as Puss sleeps at the end of my pallet.

EVERY DAY AFTER I FINISH MY MORNING CHORES, PUSS AND I hunt for rabbits. Every afternoon, I take my bounty to the butcher.

"You'll have to obtain a permit to hunt in the king's forest soon," Puss says one afternoon.

We've waited all day in the meadow behind the mill, but we've seen no hares. They're growing wise to us.

"How do you know all this, cat?" I twirl a blade of grass between my fingers.

Lying in the meadow is infinitely more comfortable in my breeches and shirt. They are worth every coin I spent, even if Eugene went pale the first time he saw me, and Thomas said I looked like an outlaw. My ivory sleeves are puffed with cuffs at the wrists, and, with my belt and boots, I feel a bit like a pirate queen. I haven't told anyone that bit of fancy— not even Puss. Especially not Puss. The cat would mock me from here to Edelmyer and back again.

I received several raised eyebrows the first few weeks, but the villagers are growing accustomed to my new outfit.

"Cats are born wise," Puss answers.

Scoffing, I roll onto my back and watch the puffy white clouds drift across the sky.

Finally, when the sun is low and the meadow shines gold, we catch a single rabbit. Hoping to make it to the butcher's shop before Sarah-Anne's father closes for the day, I hurry to Glenridge.

For once, Puss wanders back to the mill to hunt mice, leaving me alone. It's about time. I was beginning to think we were going to need another barn cat.

When I reach the butcher's shop, I find it closed. The family's likely in the back, having supper, and I don't want to interrupt them. I shift from one foot to the other, debating what I'm going to do with the rabbit.

I could go home...or I could take it to Beau.

Steeling my courage, I walk down the street. I try the chocolate shop's door, curious to see if he's perhaps working late. When it doesn't open, I knock.

I'm half-hoping he's not home. How foolish do I look, standing at the chocolatier's door with another rabbit? I've seen Beau a few times in passing, but I haven't stopped by his shop like he requested.

The door opens, and I paste a smile on my face.

"Etta." His eyes light when he sees me, and his gaze travels over my outfit. He opens the door wider, inviting me in. "What do I owe the honor?"

"I have another rabbit." As I say it, I hoist the bag in front of me.

When he smiles, my insides warm.

"Are you in need of another bag?" he asks.

"Not this time. This is purely a social call."

There's something about these new clothes that makes me feel more confident. They're patch-free, and, with my shirt tucked into my breeches, they accentuate my waist in a way that my baggy dress and apron never did. The outfit is a far cry from the gowns worn by the girls that I'm sure he's used to rubbing elbows with, but at least it makes me looks as if I have a shape.

"Is it?" He sounds pleased.

I study a painting hanging on his wall. "This time, the rabbit is a gift."

"One I'll accept only if you'll stay to share it with me."

Turning, I smile at him, happy for the company. Though I love my brothers, the mill seems to be growing smaller by the day. "Agreed."

It's long after dark when Puss announces his presence by howling at the closed window.

"It seems we have a visitor," Beau says from his side of the small table where we shared our meal.

When I open the door, I scowl at the cat. Puss saunters into the shop, and his eyes travel over the counter and art. His gaze finally lands on the table that holds the remnants of our supper.

Familiar with the wicked gleam in his eyes, I pick him up before he can leap in the middle and send the settings flying to the floor. He wriggles in my arms, but, realizing I have no intention of letting him loose, soon stops resisting.

Trapped, the cat turns his eyes on Beau and glares.

"I'm under the distinct impression that your feline doesn't like me very much," Beau says, giving Puss a wary look of his own.

"He's oddly protective of me."

Beau busies himself with clearing the table, a smile playing on his lips. "If I were yours, I'd be protective as well."

My cheeks warm, and Puss lets out a quiet hiss of indignation. I don't read too much into the flippantly-spoken words, though. Beau's been walking this line all evening. When he flashes me a not-so-subtle smile, Sarah-Anne's warning words circle in my head. But they aren't the obstacle making me hesitate from flirting back.

It's no use. No matter how handsome he is, Beau's not the man who consumes my thoughts. It would be wrong of me to lead him on.

"I should go," I say, and Puss mews in an approving manner.

Beau looks over, startled. "You don't have to rush off."

I glance out the window. "It's growing late."

"At least let me walk you home. I can't let you wander through the streets in the dark."

A smile twitches my lips. "And what will you protect me from?"

He leans against the counter. "Wolves? Giants? Witches?"

"We have none of those in sleepy Glenridge."

"Bandits...?" He scrunches his mouth to the side, thinking. Then his eyes sharpen, and he ventures, "What about ogres?"

Puss becomes too heavy, and I set him on the floor, trusting him to behave himself now that I've decided to leave.

"Wrong province," I say, grinning despite myself. "They're farther south."

Satisfied with my answer, he nods. Then, with a grin of his own, he says, "If you don't let me do my gentlemanly duty, my pride will take a hard hit."

I'm looking at my cat when he says it, and Puss winces and wrinkles his nose as if he's smelled something bad.

"Well, we can't have that," I say. "Come on, then."

With Puss leading us, I take Beau's offered arm. The streets are alight with thick, flickering flames atop candles in lampposts. Though the hour has grown late, people, after having eaten their suppers, are out, enjoying the warm summer evening. A trio of musicians play from a corner in the square, and a crowd has gathered to watch them. Children run this way and that, and I soak up the merrymaking.

We're just passing the butcher's shop when Beau abruptly attempts to change our course. Curious, I look at him, but my question is quickly answered.

The pretty eighteen-year-old daughter of the baker stops in front of us. Marissa's eyes flicker to our linked arms, and she frowns.

"Hello, Marissa," Beau says, a somewhat strained look on his face. He presses his arm closer to his side, keeping my hand firmly in place, and he bows in greeting. "Lovely to run into you."

Marissa glances at me before she answers, "You as well."

After several more slightly awkward exchanged words, we continue on. Puss takes an odd turn down a street. Since he's a good ways ahead of us, we have no choice but to follow. Not two minutes later, the scene repeats itself, this time with a farmer's daughter from the outskirts of Glenridge. She blinks several times when she spots me and Beau.

"Ah, Maria," Beau says, this time sounding acutely uncomfortable. "Pleasant evening."

41

The pretty, shy girl lowers her eyes and murmurs a quick greeting as she hurries past us.

Once she's gone, Beau clears his throat.

"You're popular," I say.

He rolls his eyes. "Since I've moved here, I feel like a prime piece of meat, hanging from the butcher's shop."

I'm reminded of Sarah-Anne's warning, but I attempt to smile. Poor girls. Before Kerrick—before I even knew Beau—I was a little lovesick over him myself.

"I'm sure I'm quite safe from ogres, giants, and witches if you'd prefer to head back to your shop and hide from your ardent admirers," I say.

Beau glances at me, surprised. "I'd prefer to walk you."

"Your shine will wear off," I assure him as we continue on. "Glenridge is a small town. You're exciting and new, but I'm sure they'll tire of you soon."

He flashes me a wry smile. "You're good on a man's ego."

"Do you think you need your ego stroked when women are falling at your feet like flies?"

Peering straight ahead, he gives me a sideways look. "Some of them don't fall at all. They offer sweet smiles and rabbits and then disappear for weeks at a time, making me wonder if I'm losing my touch."

I warm at the words, but I know it's just careless banter. Judging from the evening, it's obvious Beau didn't come to Glenridge seeking romance. But, like me, it seems he could use a friend.

"Then they show back up," he continues, turning so our gazes meet, "looking like an adventuress and smelling of sunshine."

My pride glows at the flattery, and I laugh. "See? This is your problem. If you want to deter them, you need to act aloof and disinterested. You're entirely too charming."

He grins. "I'll work on it."

"Yes." I nod. "You do that."

Beau gives me a look, and we continue on. We've left the village and its warm light behind, and we walk down the winding lane that eventually leads to the mill.

"So who is it you fancy?" Beau asks.

The question takes me by surprise. "I'm sorry?"

"You have that look about you every time you come to Glenridge—the look of a girl hoping to catch a glimpse of someone." He flashes me a lopsided smile. "Assuming it's not me?"

Ironically, at one point it had been Beau I was looking for. But that was before I met Kerrick, before I even knew Beau.

"There is no one," I answer truthfully. "But there is the hope."

He thinks about my answer for a moment, and then he nods. Shortly after, I ask him to tell me more about his travels, and we continue to the mill in comfortable conversation.

CHAPTER 8

Beau

A GUST OF WIND KICKS UP, SENDING BRANCHES SWAYING. A few green leaves fall to the ground, swirling in the breeze before they finally fall. Even the brief respite from the hot, humid day does little to lift my spirits. My horse tosses her head and surges forward, eager to race the wind. In a foul mood unsuited for a pleasure ride, I hold her back. I've been in Glenridge an entire season and have not found the slightest sign of an ogre.

And, on top of that, somehow in the course of an evening, Etta's decided we should be friends.

The sight of her on my doorstep yesterday evening sent me reeling. What kind of fools are her brothers that they allow her to wander about the woods and village in that outfit? I clench my eyes shut, trying not to picture the way she looked in her hunting breeches and boots, with her hair persistently falling from its pins and her skin kissed by the summer sun.

She looked like an adventuress, a woman not unlike those I've known on the seas—a woman indifferent to conventions and customs. One who goes wherever she pleases, whenever she pleases.

But Etta's not a woman. She's a girl, only eighteen or nineteen at the most, a few years younger than I am, and her innocent light brown eyes belie that she's not as worldly as she may now seem at first glance.

The back of my neck aches, and I rub a gloved hand over it. I'm farther south than I've traveled yet, near the boundary of this kingdom, where King Deloge's land ends and another's begins. If Etta's right, this is the province where the ogres are to be found. Yet every person I've asked gives me the same answer: "No, no, Monsieur. No ogres have been seen in these parts for tens of years." And when I ask them of my father? A man who left here only thirty years before? All I receive are blank stares and murmured apologies.

No one recognizes the name. My paternal family might as well have gone up in smoke.

Absently, I rub my ring through the layer of leather. This was supposed to be simple. I was going to sort the ogre matter out by autumn and be back at sea before winter.

I pull my horse to a stop and take in the landscape. This province is rich in farmland. Fields are lush and tall, and cattle and sheep graze the grassy slopes. The people I've met are friendly, yet all have an air of exhaustion about them. Despite the great bounty surrounding them, they are tired and hungry.

A farmer approaches in his cart, and I raise a hand in greeting. "Who owns these lands?"

The man jerks his head behind him, farther to the south. "Monsieur Mattis. He lives in the castle over yonder."

I glance in that direction, but all I see are fields, a few stretches of meadow, and patches of forest. "How long has the lord lived here?"

"His family's always been here, Monsieur. For generations."

After letting out another long, defeated breath, I ask, "I've heard talk of ogres in these parts. Have you had trouble with them?"

The man's eyebrows shoot up. "Ogres?" He laughs. "I've never heard of their likes in this province."

Frowning, I bid the man good day.

Another dead end.

CHAPTER 9

Etta

Rynvale, the village surrounding the castle, is huge. I've never seen so many people all in one place. Though we live only an hour's ride away, I've never been here.

Puss trots at my side, but I have to be careful not to speak to him lest people think I'm mad. I make my way through the crowded streets, but I'm not sure where it is I'm headed.

"Which way?" I hiss under my breath.

"Toward the castle," the cat answers, unconcerned that others may hear him.

There are so many people, it's doubtful anyone would even notice a talking cat.

Eventually, Puss leads me to the lowered drawbridge. Guards stand on either side, and peasants and merchants come and go freely. Still, I hesitate. "Are you sure I'm allowed through there?"

The cat strolls ahead of me. "Of course I'm sure."

No one says a word as we cross over the drawbridge. The castle's courtyard is even more chaotic than the village. Clusters of guards practice with rapiers and bows, and merchants have set up carts right in the pathways. Other people of varying stations mill around, browsing wares and tossing coins to the musicians and acrobats who weave through the crowd.

Puss leads me through the fray, right to the castle gates.

"What is your business?" a bored guard asks.

The sun hangs directly overhead, and the man must be overheated in his leather and the tabard he wears over his shirt.

"I've come to ask the king's permission to hunt in his forest?" I'm unsure of myself, and the statement comes out as a question.

The guard's eyes drift over me, over my breeches and boots, and he frowns. Instead of challenging me, however, he opens the doors.

I step forward, awed.

The quiet of the castle is a far cry from the commotion of the courtyard. The atmosphere is hushed, and the entry is cool. There are people here and there, some sitting on padded benches and others standing in clusters. Swords, shields, and tapestries hang on the walls. Shining suits of armor from an era long past line the entry.

I must stand gawking because a finely dressed man in official garb, a steward, strides forward to greet me.

"What is your business?" he asks.

I blink at him, overwhelmed, and I tell him why I'm here. He efficiently herds me down a hall to the direct right, and soon I'm in an area that's bare of decoration.

A man sits behind a scarred wooden desk, and he's speaking with a nobleman. The steward who escorted me motions that the seated man is the one I need to speak with, and I hang back until he's finished. Puss sits at my feet, and his tail flicks back and forth as if he has deemed himself too important to wait.

The man in front of me finally turns to leave. Noting his rank, I lower my eyes out of respect and step forward.

"Good afternoon," the nobleman says when he notices me.

Recognizing the voice, I jerk my chin up. There, in front of me, after all this time, is Kerrick.

His blond hair is even lighter than it was this spring, faded after hours in the sun, and his skin is quite tan. Just like the first day I met him, he's dressed well, but he carries himself in a casual sort of way. As if he's very comfortable in his own skin.

"Hello," I answer, feeling light.

With nothing more than a warm smile and a brief glance at my unconventional clothing, he's out the door.

He doesn't remember me.

My heart freezes and then shatters. After all this time, after all these hours thinking of him, he doesn't remember.

And why would he?

"Can I help you?" the man behind the desk asks, startling me from my brooding. After I state my business, he says, "That will be two gold coins."

I suck in a surprised breath. Two gold coins just for permission to hunt in the king's forest? That's absurd. It would take me an entire season of catching rabbits to earn that much.

Stunned, I begin to shake my head and back away. As I murmur my apologies for wasting his time, I glare at Puss.

"You dropped these," a voice says from behind my shoulder.

I turn, and there he is again. Kerrick stands in front of me, two gold coins in his hand.

"I thought you left," I say.

A crooked smile tips his lips. "I remembered something."

His eyebrows raise with expectation, and he extends his hand a little farther.

"Those aren't mine," I say, my embarrassment growing.

"Of course they are."

The man behind the desk, looking amused as well as exasperated, clears his throat and holds his own hand up, ready to receive the coins. After Kerrick hands them to him, the man scratches on a bit of parchment. "Your permit, mademoiselle. Just sign your name."

For the first time, I'm truly glad my father taught me to read and write before he passed. I sign the parchment and then accept it when the man hands it to me.

Satisfied, the clerk nods and looks away, dismissing me.

"Thank you," I murmur to Kerrick as I clutch the permit close.

With nothing else to say, I step past him. When I turn to leave, he follows. Uncomfortable, I hurry along until he places his hand on my arm.

"You don't remember me, do you?" His blue eyes are bright with good humor.

How could anyone forget a man with eyes like that?

"Did your father like the book?" I ask instead of directly answering him.

A quick smile flashes across his face, but he quickly subdues it. "He did."

We continue walking, and I try not to fidget. First, I cross my arms. Then, feeling foolish, I let them drop to my sides. Puss stays at my heel, thankfully silent.

"I wouldn't have guessed you to be a huntress," he finally says.

I glance at my cat, looking for answers. Puss yawns.

Apparently, he'll be no help.

"I'm learning." For the first time, I'm self-conscious in my breeches. Yes, they fit well. But in front of Kerrick, they feel scandalous.

As if sensing my discomfort, he motions to my outfit and says, "The occupation suits you."

My cheeks grow hot, and I purse my lips to trap in a nervous giggle.

We leave the castle and step into the courtyard. I shield my eyes from the bright sunlight as they adjust. It's another hot, sunny day.

"I could teach you a bit if you like." Then, sounding as if he's striving to be humble, he adds, "I'm rather skilled myself."

Lowering my hand, I turn to Kerrick. "You would?"

At that, Puss butts his head against my leg and yowls. I shake him away.

After giving the cat a questioning look, Kerrick looks back at me and nods.

He isn't handsome in the same way Beau is. Kerrick is like one of the elves of the eastern forests, perfect and golden. The two men are both tall and lean, but there's a softness about Kerrick, a perfectness. As my eyes travel his face, I absently note that his bottom lip is just ever so slightly fuller than his top.

Daydreams flit to my mind, and I blink the thoughts away before he catches me staring at him like a besotted fool.

I clear my throat. "I'd like that."

"I'm leaving tomorrow to visit my uncle," he says. "But I'll meet you next week?"

"All right."

"Noon? Where the road meets the king's forest?" he asks.

I nod.

As he turns to leave, I stop him. "Who are you?"

He glances at the castle and then back at me. "No one of importance."

"I doubt that." Setting my hands on my hips, I give him a wry smile.

He wrinkles his nose as if he doesn't care for the question. "I'm the fifth son of a minor lord."

So he may be from money, but there's no title in his future. I'm not sure why, but that soothes my worries.

I smile. "Until next week."

Surprising me, he takes my hand and brushes his lips over my knuckles. "I'll be looking forward to it."

WE'RE HALFWAY HOME, AND PUSS ISN'T SPEAKING WITH ME.

"I thought you wanted me to learn to hunt," I finally say, teasing. "Isn't the skill fundamental to your great master plan for our lives?"

Instead of staying on the road, we've taken a shortcut through a meadow. I wind through the wildflowers, plucking a few as we go and twisting them into a tiny crown.

"I can teach you everything you need to know."

Leaning forward, I set the tiny crown on the cat's head. It sits lopsided over one ear, and he shakes it off, looking particularly put out as he knocks the ring to the ground.

"You don't think a human can learn better from another human?"

"You'll need a bow," Puss huffs, ignoring my question. "I doubt the boy will be impressed with your bag."

I smile foolishly as I hop on a boulder in my path and then jump off the other side. As happy as I am, part of me is worried I dreamed the whole meeting. Perhaps I'll wait for Kerrick, and he'll never come. I'll be heartbroken.

My thoughts shift from euphoric to terrified and then back again.

"Where will I find a bow?" I ask, trying to chase away the dark thoughts.

The cat trots ahead, probably worried I'll try to decorate him again. "A master bowyer lives out here, on the outskirts of Rynvale. You will speak with him."

It's now that I realize Puss has been leading me off course. A merry little cottage grows in the distance. Black and white dairy cows graze in a fenced-in pasture. Chickens peck the ground, and ducks waddle down the lane.

A man sits under the shade of a tree, shaping a longbow. When he sees me approaching, he stands.

With my cat gone mute, I explain my business.

"Have you ever shot a bow?" the man who introduces himself as Samuel asks, studying me. He's a good ten years older than Eugene, his hair is brown, bleached from the sun, and the skin at the corners of his eyes is wrinkled as if he smiles often.

I shift my weight, uncomfortable. "No."

Samuel rubs a hand over his chin. "You'd be better with a lightweight crossbow, I believe, but they're more expensive."

Glancing at Puss, frowning, I ask, "How expensive?"

"Are you any good with a needle?" he asks.

I nod.

"My wife's in Primsbell, visiting her sister, and I've ripped my riding cloak. Mend it for me, and I'll give you a crossbow." My face must light up because he warns, "It's old, mind you. But it should serve your purposes just fine."

"Thank you," I say, my spirits lifting.

With the bowyer's cloak tucked securely under my arm, Puss and I walk the rest of the way back to the mill.

CHAPTER 10

Beau

"THE PROCESS IS ACTUALLY—" I STOP MID-SENTENCE BECAUSE Etta has just rounded the corner of the street. She hasn't seen me yet, but it's only a matter of time.

She hurries forward, lost in thought, a full bag over her shoulder. As usual, she's rushing to the butcher's before he closes shop for the night.

"Monsieur Marchand?" the sundry shopkeeper's daughter, Lilianna, prods. "You were saying?"

I look back at the girl and her group of friends who surrounded me for a chat in the street as I was walking to the butcher's shop myself, hoping to catch Etta.

"Yes, er, chocolate," I continue. "As I was saying, it's a simple process…"

Etta looks up as she draws close. Her eyes sweep over the gaggle of girls, and she hides a teasing smile.

Distracted, I murmur, "Would you excuse me?"

The girls protest, but I brush past them as politely as possible to meet Etta.

She gives me a sideways look as I match her pace. "Those girls all hate me now."

I don't dare glance over my shoulder to see if they're watching us, but I can feel them stare daggers at our backs, so I'm sure she's right. I shrug, not overly concerned. "Disappointment's part of life."

"Perhaps it would be beneficial to everyone if you would hang a plaque about your neck stating that you're not in Glenridge looking for romance." Though she's trying to keep a straight face, an ornery smile plays at her lips.

I choose to ignore that particular statement. "Come riding with me tomorrow. I'm going to close my shop for the day."

She glances over and raises a brow. "Riding? I'm afraid my family only has a donkey, and he's not the noble steed he believes himself to be."

I wait a moment. "You could ride with me."

We've just reached the butcher's shop and Etta turns, smiling. "Imagine how people would gossip. I'm afraid it doesn't matter anyway—I have plans tomorrow."

"Plans?" I ask, smiling as I cross my arms. "Are you weeding the garden? Doing the wash?"

She gives me a wry smile. "I'm meeting a...friend."

After she says it, a funny look passes over her face, but it's soon dismissed. She pats my arm, much like I imagine she would her brothers. "Perhaps another time."

With a wave, she walks into the butcher's shop, and I'm left standing on the street, looking like a fool.

CHAPTER 11

Etta

He's not going to come.

Even Puss thinks it, but the cat hasn't said anything yet. Instead, he sits on a rock near the road that leads into the king's forest, his tail twitching as if he knows this is a waste of our time.

I adjust the cuff on my right wrist, center the buckle of my belt, and then I pace a little ways into the forest only to walk back out again. My new crossbow feels odd over my shoulder blades. Though Samuel said it was light compared to most, it still feels heavy. Still, the bowyer promised I'd become accustomed to the weight of it.

I'm again walking into the shadow of the forest when the faint sound of hoofbeats reaches my ears. I turn, eager—but trying not to look too eager. Every muscle in my body relaxes when I see him.

Kerrick rides down the road at a fast pace, and his bay horse glistens in the sun. Even I can tell it's a magnificent animal, and I don't know a thing about horses. I perch on the rock next to Puss, hoping to look carefree—as if it mattered little to me whether he came or not.

"I apologize," he says, dismounting as soon as he reaches us. "I was held up."

I give him a smile, a smile that says I hadn't even noticed, and stand. I clasp my hands in front of me, and then, feeling foolish, I cross my arms.

He looks good, as always, today dressed for the hunt. His doublet is a dark rich green, and his breeches are brown. The colors bring out the green in his eyes, making them lighter in contrast. In the shade of the forest, his hair appears darker.

Kerrick glances about. "Did you walk?"

I nod, almost hating to admit we don't own a horse. I certainly wasn't going to borrow Thomas's wretched donkey.

He raises an eyebrow at Puss. "I see you brought your cat again."

"There's no getting rid of him." I flash Puss a teasing grin. "He follows me everywhere."

Still on the rock, Puss stares at me and slowly settles to his belly. He thinks meeting with Kerrick is a waste of time, and the only reason he's here is to humor me. Oddly, he doesn't seem to have a problem with the man himself. The cat's only indignant that I'm taking hunting lessons from someone other than him.

When Kerrick and I run out of pleasantries, we head into the forest. He walks his horse, staying by my side, and we try to fill in the awkward stretches of silence.

"When did you decide to become a huntress?" he asks after we've walked for some time.

Slowly, it becomes more comfortable between us, and I no longer seem to be as conscious of my hands.

I study a patch of dainty white wildflowers ahead of us. "I began trapping rabbits and found the butcher will pay a decent price for them. Our field has done poorly in the last few years, and it's been difficult making ends meet."

"And your brothers?" he asks, remembering them from the first day we met. "What do they do?"

"Eugene takes care of the mill, and Thomas helps him and finds odd jobs where he can. I expect he'll be looking for an apprenticeship in Rynvale before long. He's a gifted whittler." I toy with my belt buckle, running my fingers over the cold metal. "Eugene will marry by the time the year is over, I'm sure."

I can feel Kerrick glance at me, but I don't look over.

"And you?" he finally asks. "Will you marry soon?"

The truth is, no one's asked me. I don't fancy any of the villagers, and they all know I have no dowry. And in a village the size of Glenridge, my options are slim. Marcus, the blacksmith's son, is still unwed, but he's eight years older than I am and always covered in soot. Not that there's anything wrong with that, exactly, but it doesn't appeal to me.

Simon, the tailor's nephew and apprentice, is handsome but a widower. His young wife died early last winter, and he's kept to himself ever since.

And Beau...well, there's certainly no future there. Half a dozen heartbroken girls in the village can attest to that.

"I have no immediate plans," I answer after a moment that lasted a heartbeat too long.

Kerrick, ever the gentleman, drops the subject.

"My life is dull," I say after he asks more about the mill. "Tell me of yours."

He makes a low, thoughtful sound in the back of his throat. "I'm not sure mine is terribly interesting."

"I doubt that." I glance at him. "Tell me the most interesting thing there is to know about you."

A slow smile builds on his lips. "I slew a dragon last summer. My first."

"Did you?" I ask, impressed. "Truly?"

We've wandered from the main road, taken a deer trail deeper into the woods. Birds call to each other from the forest canopy, and squirrels chase each other up thick, gnarled trunks. It's beautiful here, peaceful.

"The beast spent the season terrorizing the shepherdesses of Garpen—swooping down and snatching sheep, burning their fields."

"What did you do?" I ask.

He grins. "Tracked it to its lair and vanquished the beast."

"Impressive."

Every once in a while as we walk, Kerrick kneels, studies several tracks, and then motions me down another animal trail. He explains what he's doing, but I honestly can't pay attention when his eyes are on me. As loud as we are, I doubt we'll sneak up on anything anyway.

Once again, Kerrick stoops to the ground. "I've told you mine. Now you must tell me what's the most interesting thing there is to know about you."

I frown. The most interesting thing would be that I have a talking cat, but that just makes me sound mad.

After several moments, I shrug. "I'm afraid there is nothing interesting about me. Nothing at all."

"I find that hard to believe." He runs his eyes over my unusual outfit, incredulous.

Thankfully, Kerrick spots something as we near a clearing, and I don't have to explain just how dull my life truly is. Let him think there's something mysterious about me if he wants.

Kerrick ties his horse to a tree, crouches down, and waves me over. There, grazing on the sweet meadow grass, is a quartet of does. I blink at them, startled. We actually found something.

Somehow, they haven't heard us yet. As I kneel next to Kerrick, the closest shifts her large ears toward us and raises her head. We stay still as she angles in our direction. After several moments, she lowers her head again. Puss watches the deer with interest, his eyes bright. I know he realizes he hasn't a chance, but I run my hand down his back as a reminder.

"Go ahead," Kerrick whispers to me.

I angle toward him. "I thought you were here to teach me."

He glances at the crossbow on my back. "She's right there —just aim for her shoulder."

Right there.

I can't do it.

"I've never shot the bow," I admit.

Kerrick gives me an incredulous look. "What do you mean you've never shot it?"

Growing frustrated, I say, "I mean I traded the bowyer for it yesterday. I don't even know how to load an arrow."

He grimaces and shakes his head, but a smile plays at his lips as he gives me a sideways look. "Perhaps this hunting lesson should become a shooting lesson."

Nodding, I stand. The deer spook and dart into the trees across the meadow. Unable to help himself, Puss runs after them. Once they disappear from sight, he sits in the middle of the field, proud of himself—but for what, I can't imagine.

I shake my head, wondering how a talking cat like Puss can seem just as feline as the rest of his dimwitted kind at times.

Turning my attention to Kerrick and pointing to my bow, I say, "Where do we start?"

WE BEGIN THE LESSON WITH THE BEST OF INTENTIONS, BUT the warm day sabotages us. By mid-afternoon I find myself lying next to Kerrick on the meadow grass, staring at the clouds as they float by. Hot from the sun, the wildflowers emit the smell of summer all around us.

Puss, after looking disgusted with me for most of the day, now naps not far away. Every once in a while, he stretches a tawny leg, yawns wide, and then rolls to his other side, perfectly content.

"I think it looks like a duck," I say.

Kerrick laughs, disagreeing. "A duck? How do you possibly get any kind of fowl out of that?"

Grinning, pointing above us at the cloud, I say, "There's his beak, and there"—I move my finger—"is his tail."

"I still don't see it." Kerrick rolls to his side, facing me. "I've never done this."

"You've never made shapes from the clouds?" I roll toward him as well. There's still an arm's length of room between us, but it's as close to a man as I've ever been. My heart warms, and my stomach flutters. My worries of my future, of Eugene and Sarah-Anne—they're all forgotten for the moment, and I'm blissfully happy.

He shakes his head, and a slow, lazy grin spreads across his face. "Never."

I move my arm underneath me, propping it up so I can rest my head on my palm as I look at him. "Then how do you pass summer afternoons?"

Matching my stance, he says, "I ride, read, fight...*hunt*."

"Don't say that word. It makes me feel guilty, like there's something better we should be doing."

"What do you do, Suzette?" He says my name like a caress. "On hot summer afternoons when you're not painting pictures in the sky?"

"That was very poetic."

"Tell no one."

I smile at his grimace. "What would I be doing? Rather,

61

what I *should* be doing. Baking bread, weeding the vegetable patch, tending to the mending." I let out a long sigh. "Trapping rabbits."

Out of nowhere, Kerrick says, "Has anyone ever told you how beautiful your hair is?"

My heart leaps, and I turn my eyes back to his. "No."

Slowly, as if he's afraid I'll dart away, he takes a light brown strand and winds it around his hand. "It's like gold."

"Only in the sun." My voice is breathy.

"Whenever I look back on this day, I will remember you as the embodiment of what a summer should be." He pauses as his eyes move from my hair to my eyes. "Bright, warm, beautiful."

He's inching forward, ever so slowly. Finding courage, I lean in as well.

Inches from me, he stops and clenches his eyes shut. "I'm sorry."

"For what?" I breathe.

Kerrick opens his eyes. "For letting myself get carried away."

I take a deep breath and slowly let it out of my nose. My whole body deflates with it. I cover my disappointment with an understanding expression and again roll onto my back.

"But why not?" Kerrick suddenly says. He closes the distance between us, and, without hesitation, lowers his lips to mine. My heart leaps in my chest. Tentative, suddenly shy, I set my hands on his sun-warmed shoulders. Tiny bits of weeds and dirt cling to his doublet, but I couldn't care less.

"Tomorrow," he promises as he pulls back just slightly.

Catching my breath, I say, "Tomorrow what?"

Grinning, he presses another soft kiss to my lips. "Tomorrow I'll teach you how to shoot."

CHAPTER 12

THE SUMMER DAYS PASS TOO QUICKLY NOW THAT I'M MEETING Kerrick in the king's forest every afternoon. No one except Puss knows. It's our secret alone. Even the cat gives us privacy, going off to hunt mice and rabbits while we linger, laughing in the meadow, watching the clouds, sharing stolen kisses.

My brothers, though not terribly observant, have noticed my absences. Eugene, however, is happy to spend more private time with Sarah-Anne, and Thomas has, indeed, taken a carpentry apprenticeship in Rynvale that keeps him away in the afternoon hours. But every once in a while, when I return just a little too late, the two look at me with hawkish stares, wondering if I'm up to more in the woods than trapping rabbits.

Like my cat, I stay mute on the subject.

Though Kerrick and I have never discussed it, I know our time is limited. He's made no promises, never even hinted at it. But I long for him to. Every day I hope that this may be the afternoon he says he wants me forever, no matter the consequences. But I know. I know.

I have him now, and, somehow, that has to be enough.

In the evenings, when I rejoin my cat, we make our way back to the mill, and I capture rabbits in my bag. I still haven't used my crossbow.

Puss assures me I'll grow used to it, but I'm not sure. I have, however, become quite proficient at trapping.

I swing my bag back and forth as I stroll into Glenridge with Puss at my heels. Kerrick had to be home early today, and for once, I'm not rushing into the village to catch the butcher before he closes shop.

It's another market day, and the town is bustling. I greet villagers as I walk through the streets, exchanging pleasantries when people stop.

"Etta," a smooth, masculine voice says from behind me.

I turn, my lips already twitching with a smile. "Hello, Beau."

The chocolatier looks as good as always, and I notice a few girls give him wistful looks as he passes. He tips his hat to them but hurries past.

"You're a terrible friend," he says with a smile when he finally turns his attention back to me.

Tossing my bag over my shoulder, unconcerned, I say, "Why is that?"

He matches my pace, and, together we walk down the crowded street toward the butcher's. "I've barely seen you these last few weeks."

"I saw you the day before yesterday," I remind him.

We both know that it was in passing, as it usually is these days, and I didn't have time to speak with him because the butcher was about to close.

"What's kept you so busy?" he asks.

I shake my head as he, again, is stopped by a pretty young girl, this time, the chandler's niece. When the girl has passed, I say, "It's none of your business."

At the tone of my voice, Beau turns back to me. Both amused and curious, he says, "You could make it my business."

He ends up following me all the way to the butcher's shop and doesn't seem to have any intention of leaving. I come out of the door with my money pouch heavier than when I went in and find him leaning against the wall, waiting.

Beau nods down the street, toward his shop. "I'll bribe you with chocolate if you'll tell me."

I think about it for a moment. It would be nice to tell someone besides Puss, who's a little too condescending at times.

The cat flicks his gaze at me, whiskers twitching as if he can tell what I'm thinking.

Giving Puss an ornery smile, I finally nod to Beau. "All right, but only for chocolate."

Puss hisses low, but I choose to ignore him.

We arrive at the shop, and, again, Beau makes the hot chocolate drink. After I take my first long sip, I tell him my story.

"And you have no idea who this man is?" Beau asks.

I shake my head and swirl the drink in my hand. "It doesn't make any difference. It won't last."

It's easy to talk to Beau, likely because he's too disinterested in gossip to judge my fleeting summer affair.

Beau frowns. "Just be careful."

Tilting my head, I give him a wry look. "Do you have any idea how many times I've heard that in the last season?"

"It's sage advice," Beau argues.

"Yes, well that might be," I say, my smile growing. "But the first few times I heard it, it was in correlation to *you*."

His light green eyes brighten. "Oh really? And what exactly brought about that conversation?"

I laugh at his teasing and take another sip of the chocolate drink.

Beau looks at the darkening sky. "It's growing late. Will you join me for supper?"

With a sigh, I push away from the table. "No, I should be going. I've made my brothers fend for themselves too many times this week."

As I'm leaving, Beau catches my arm. "Don't stay away so long next time."

My heart swells with warmth, and I grasp his hand. "I've never had a friend. I'm so happy you settled here."

His mouth quirks to the side. When I think he's going to say something, he only squeezes my hand and nods. After I send Beau one last wave, Puss and I leave the chocolate shop.

CHAPTER 13

Beau

JUST AS ETTA'S ABOUT TO TURN DOWN THE NEXT STREET, SHE glances back and sends me one last wave. I hold my hand up, smiling like I don't want to track down this mysterious man and interrogate him. Or…make him disappear altogether.

But no.

I can't do anything of the sort because Etta has decided we are *friends*.

Growling under my breath, I lean against the door and close my eyes.

"Monsieur Marchand!" Marissa calls from down the street. "Good evening, Monsieur!"

That growl becomes a groan. I push against the door, tip my hat to the young woman, and escape inside before she grows close enough to corner me.

Why is it that every girl in the village is practically stalking me except for the one I wish would?

"Friends." I shake my head and close the door behind me.

CHAPTER 14

As I always seem to be when I visit Beau's shop, I arrive home later than planned. It's twilight when I reach the mill. I pause on the step, looking out over the field. The wheat is tall. Eugene was right. It's been a good season.

With the late summer harvest, he should have enough to wed Sarah-Anne.

And I need to be out of his way so he'll ask her.

"Why are you gawking?" Thomas calls from the pasture.

I turn toward him, surprised that I didn't see him there. He grins and points across the fence. There, standing where the old, contrary donkey should be, is a horse. She's not young or fine, but she's sturdy and quite handsome.

"How did you manage that?" I ask.

"I paid for her." He's obviously proud of himself. "I sold twenty-three figurines to a merchant traveling through Rynvale today. He said he'll sell them in Edelmyer, and from there they'll be shipped across the seas. Can you imagine that?"

Lighting up at the news, I walk toward him to inspect the mare better. "Did you really? Thomas, that's wonderful!"

He bites his lip and nods. "Etta."

The strange quality of his voice startles me, and I give him my full attention. "What's wrong?"

"I'm moving to Rynvale after the harvest."

All the air whooshes from my lungs, and I have to look away so he won't see how his news has affected me. I knew it was coming. I hadn't expected it quite this soon.

"Of course you should." Once I'm sure of myself, I give him a big smile. "It's foolish to travel back and forth every day."

"Etta..."

I wave his concern away. "I'm happy for you."

"You'll be fine," he says quietly. "You've met someone, haven't you? That's where you go during the day, why you come back all starry-eyed and nauseating."

For some reason, my brother's usual teasing in that *unusually* concerned tone, makes my eyes sting. I don't trust my voice, so I give him a vague shrug—one that I'm hoping he'll interpret as secretive.

He waits a moment, as if he wants to say something but doesn't know how to go about it. Finally, he says, "It's not Beau...is it?"

Startled, I laugh out loud. "No, it's most certainly not Beau."

At that, Thomas nods, obviously relieved. "Good."

We stand together, side by side, studying his new horse. After several quiet minutes, Eugene pokes his head out the door. "What are you two doing?" He grins. "Etta, I'm starving. Please tell me you have an idea what's for supper."

Thomas clasps my shoulder, gives me a grin, and then we head into the mill.

EUGENE AND THOMAS ARE HARVESTING THE WHEAT TODAY. IT'S the end of the summer, and the day feels ominous. The weather is still hot, but this morning there was the chill of autumn in the air. Kerrick is quiet, somewhat withdrawn.

I aim at a large "X" that Kerrick carved into a dead tree the day we began our lessons. It's become my practice target. The arrow slices through the air and hits the tree with a satisfying thud. I lower the crossbow.

"This is my closest yet," I say as I examine the hit.

Kerrick looks at it and nods, satisfied. "You're a consistent shot now."

"Not bad considering five weeks ago I couldn't hit the tree."

He laughs, but his mind is obviously elsewhere.

The sun is low, and it's nearing the time we usually part.

"Are we finished?" I ask softly. When I say the words, I mean for the day. But that's not how they sound. That's not how he takes them.

Kerrick freezes. After watching me for several moments, he glances at the sky. The birds have already quieted in the trees, and the shadows are growing long.

"I'm going to be late as it is," he finally says, choosing not to answer the deeper question.

"Late for what?" I hoist my crossbow onto my back. My arms, though more muscular than they were when we started our lessons, are exhausted from holding the bow all afternoon. I stretch my sore neck from one side to the other, trying to keep things light between us.

Looking uncomfortable, Kerrick wrinkles his nose. "Just a…gathering of sorts. Something my father planned."

There's something about the way he says it that makes my heart feel as if it's stopped beating.

"What kind of gathering?" My voice is a little too quiet.

Kerrick won't look at me. Then, in a rush, he answers,

"My father has decided it's time I should marry. Apparently, he believes I'm too incompetent to choose my own bride, so he's searching for one for me."

There it is.

I've known it was coming, knew it's what our future held, but I still can't breathe.

Somehow, I plaster a nonchalant smile on my face and nod. Pulling a leaf from a nearby tree and studying it, I say, "A lot of fuss for a fifth son."

For one split second, he meets my eyes, and then he looks away. He clears his throat, but when I expect him to continue, he stays silent.

"I should go too." I nod toward the south, toward Glenridge.

Kerrick looks lost for words, and for once, strikingly vulnerable. His voice husky, he says, "Don't—"

"Thank you," I say, and then I gulp as my throat thickens. "For teaching me to shoot."

Somehow I know I won't see him again, and my chest feels as if an iron weight has been placed on it.

"Suzette, wait," Kerrick says, though he appears to be glued to the forest floor. When I turn back, he continues, "You have to understand—I have no choice in the matter. It's a burden, sometimes, being born of noble blood."

My cheeks grow warm. "It must be hard on you to always know you'll have a place to live…to have food on the table." I try to soften my words with a smile, but my heart isn't into it.

Kerrick's eyebrows knit, and he clears his throat again, this time, embarrassed. "This was selfish of me, and I am sorry—so truly, deeply sorry. But, for once, I wanted to spend time with someone I was actually interested in getting to know. To do something just because it made me happy."

Trying to stand tall, trying to look as if his words haven't affected me at all, I put on a smile. "And did you enjoy yourself?"

His eyes, those beautiful eyes, search mine, trying to convey something, but for the life of me, I don't know what. His lips turn in a frown as if he feels bad for what he's about to say. "I did, Suzette. I truly did. And I don't regret one moment I shared with you."

"Me either," I whisper, quiet enough I'm not sure if he can hear me. I turn again and walk five paces before I stop. My back still facing him, I say, "Do you remember when you asked me what the most interesting thing that's ever happened to me was?"

He makes a soft noise of affirmation, a noise of anguish.

I glance over my shoulder, this time giving him a smile that's meant to ease his guilt, to let him know I have no ill will toward him. A smile that shreds my insides and makes me feel as if my heart will bleed dry.

Blinking just once, I say, "I met you."

CHAPTER 15

Etta

PUSS DOESN'T SAY A WORD TO ME ON THE WAY HOME, AND I don't attempt to initiate a conversation. Tears run down my face. Angry, I swipe them away.

It's not that I'm in love with Kerrick. I'm not. But it would have been so easy to let myself slip.

My one consolation is that I didn't.

Thomas and Eugene exchange startled glances when I step into the mill. Ignoring them, I look at the floor. Attempting to hide my blotchy face with my hair, I climb up the ladder to my section of the loft. I heave my crossbow aside, and it falls harmlessly to the floor. In the bare privacy of my pallet, I lie face-down on the soft, age-worn blankets and cry. They're selfish tears, selfish because I know Kerrick's better off with a rich girl with a grand dowry, someone who comes to him with an equal share. But deep down, so deep I've barely admitted it to myself, I wanted him to choose me.

Puss settles next to me. When I ignore him, he crawls on my back and begins to purr.

"Get off of me, cat," I say through a mouthful of blanket.

"Be quiet." He begins to knead my shoulders with the tiny pads of his feet. "I'm comforting you."

I snort out a mirthless laugh and shake him off. "I don't want to be comforted."

Puss butts the back of my neck and then nudges in next to me. I move my head to the other side. Dauntless, he sticks his furry face in mine, forcing me to acknowledge him. Finally, tired of fighting him, I roll to my side. He settles to his belly, facing me, his tawny face looking a bit like a wildcat in the dim light.

"Cry for now, if you must," he says. "But, tomorrow, we have things to do."

With a sigh, knowing he won't go away, I open my arms to him.

I hold the cat like a child holds a doll and let silent tears fall into his fur. Normally, he'd protest, a feline far too above such treatment. But tonight he snuggles closer.

"What does it say about me that my dearest friend is a cat?" I whisper as I begin to drift.

"It says you have the very best taste in companions."

Finally, with an almost-smile on my lips, I find sleep.

CHAPTER 16

Beau

I KNOW SOMETHING'S HAPPENED THE MOMENT ETTA ARRIVES on my doorstep, but she seems determined not to speak of it, and I don't press. Still, sick as it might be, I'm hoping this mystery man of the woods has moved on.

Her eyes, which are usually so bright, are dull from a restless night. She didn't even bother to pull her hair up this morning, and now it cascades down her back in soft, unruly waves. I want to slide my hands in it, stroke her pale cheeks. Pull her close and—

I cross my arms to keep my hands where they belong.

Since she probably won't tell me what's wrong if I demand it first thing, I decide to be casual about it. Leaning a shoulder on the door frame, I raise an eyebrow in a way that usually makes her smile. "And what brings you by so early?"

Not quite meeting my eyes, Etta hikes a shoulder, listless. "I had a free morning."

Etta never has a free morning. She's too busy taking care of her brothers—all while they're busy worrying about what to do with her.

I frown, lost in my own thoughts. Why hasn't one of these

Glenridge boys asked to court her? She's old enough, especially here in this little village. It's only a matter of time, of that I'm sure. It's easy to imagine her here, playing wife to some poor farm boy.

The thought makes me uncomfortable, which is ridiculous as I barely know her.

I barely know her.

Turning so she won't see me scowl, I walk to the kitchen. Mother calls this thing attempting to plague me 'calf love;' Father called it 'infatuation.' I've seen it before, in friends and cousins. Perfectly level-headed men—smart, logical members of nobility—claiming love at first sight one day only to be broken the next. It's a disease of the heart that lasts but a season, and I'm almost certain it's all Etta is suffering from right now. She doesn't really love this man. From the conversations we've had, I don't think she even knows him.

To busy myself, I mix milk with chocolate and set it to heat. As I work, I glance at Etta. She sits at the table, her odd tawny cat in her lap, and she stares at her hands. Her eyes glisten, and she blinks quickly as if chasing tears away.

My chest tightens in the most uncomfortable way, but I clench my jaw, choosing to ignore the sensation.

I set a cup of chocolate in front of her, and, in the most nonchalant, carefree way possible, I say, "Now, tell me what's wrong."

CHAPTER 17

Etta

"I don't see what trapping a rabbit has to do with us moving up in the world," I whisper to Puss as I wait for the fat hare to make his way to my bag.

Puss woke me this morning, explaining that today was the day we put his plan in motion. Then he led me here to trap rabbits.

Again.

"Stop talking," the cat hisses.

I roll my eyes and wait, rope in hand. We've bagged three this morning already, but Puss has rejected them all. He's waiting for the perfect one—this one, apparently—to succumb to our trap. He's large for a reason. The rabbit is far more cautious than the others, and though he's obviously tempted by the tender greens from my garden, he keeps pausing.

His nose works, and his eyes dart this way and that. I'm surprised he hasn't fled already.

As I lie in the grass, hidden by several mounds of daisies, an itch tickles the skin at my hairline. I wrinkle my forehead, knowing I can't move or I'll scare the rabbit away.

And if I do that, Puss will be in a horrible temper. There's nothing more trying than a miffed feline.

Just when I think I can bear it no longer, the rabbit hops into my bag. With a yank, I jump to my feet and pull the bag closed. Puss, as always, finishes the creature. I simply don't have the stomach for it.

"There." A satisfied glint lights the cat's peridot-green eyes. "Now we go to the king."

Glancing at the bag, I frown. "What would he want with a rabbit? Surely he dines on venison and quail every night."

"I know what I'm doing," Puss argues. He's already sauntering toward the road that leads to Rynvale.

"What about the other three?" I ask.

Puss stops, and then, looking particularly put out, he changes direction and heads toward Glenridge. "Fine. We'll take them to the butcher first." He eyes me. "You need extra gold for a hat, anyway."

"A hat?"

"Something to obscure your hair and eyes."

Without further explanation, he trots toward the nearby village. I toss a hand up in the air, mildly exasperated, and follow him.

After the butcher pays me for the rabbits, I turn toward the tailor's shop, hoping he may have a suitable hat.

With no one nearby, Puss says, "Not here."

I want to ask him where he expects me to go if not the tailor's, but I don't dare while we're here on the street where someone may see me. Instead, I follow him out of Glenridge.

In the quiet of the late morning, with the sun growing warm on my shoulders and the smell of late-season wildflowers in the air, my mind wanders to Kerrick. It's not the first time today, not even close, but it's the first time I haven't had something to distract me.

Puss runs ahead, a cat on a mission, and I trail behind, not as eager to reach Rynvale.

"You'll buy a cavalier hat," the cat instructs when we near the large village.

With Puss's instructions in my head, I browse the milliner's shop. The cavalier hats are grander than I'm comfortable with. They have large brims with one side tilted high, and each boast a long plumed feather. Even the cheapest will strip me of most of my savings. I bite my lip, thinking.

The milliner comes forward, cheerful, and rests a hip against the display. "Are you sure you wouldn't care for the women's hats, mademoiselle?"

I glance at him, my lips pursed to the side in concentration. "No."

He raises a questioning eyebrow, the hint of a good humor in his expression. "The last woman I sold one of these to was a notorious outlaw."

"You say that like you don't think I could possibly be one."

The man shrugs, smiling.

"I'll take this one," I finally say, picking up the least expensive of my options.

"Let's make sure it feels right, shall we?" The milliner carefully sets the hat on my head, and then he smiles. "It rather suits you."

I feel ridiculous, but I keep the thought to myself and pay him.

When I leave the shop, Puss isn't where I left him. I wait for several minutes and then curse under my breath when he fails to reappear. The rabbit won't wait forever. It's already a hot day. I suppose I'll have to do this on my own.

The path to the castle is disconcertingly familiar. The last time we were here, I ran into Kerrick. I look for him as I walk, telling myself it's only so I can slip away if I spot him.

Mostly I just want to catch a glimpse of him—which is so very pathetic.

Sighing, I stride through the crowded streets. With my pirate queen outfit complete, I must carry an air of importance because people part for me. Some gawk, and many men even raise appreciative eyebrows. Part of me flushes with pride. Another part doesn't like to be so conspicuous.

I pass over the drawbridge without hesitation this time and present myself at the castle's entry like I belong here. There is a line today, and I wait my turn.

"Suzette," a voice hisses from the shadows near me. Surprised, I glance over and find Puss. Irritated, I leave my place and slip around the corner.

In the safety of the shadows I ask him, "Where did you disappear to?"

"What do you think you're doing?"

I shake the bag, looking at him as if he's gone daft. "I'm giving the king the rabbit."

"And who, pray tell, were you going to say it was from?"

Brushing a stray hair back under my hat, I shrug. "From myself, I suppose."

He shakes his head, an almost human move, disgusted. "No, no."

"Well, who do you want me to say it's from, cat?" I demand.

Puss jumps on the shoulder-height garden wall next to me. "You will say it's from the Marquise of Carabas."

"And who is she?"

His tail twitches with impatience. "You, eventually."

"You think the king will believe I'm a marquise?" I wave a hand over the clothes that make most people mistake me for a bandit or an adventuress.

Puss hisses, put out that I'm being so difficult. "You will go on her behalf. When I'm finished, he'll never connect the two of you. Just keep your head down, your hair up, and your eyes shadowed."

A headache blooms at the base of my neck, and I lean back to stare at the parapets. "I don't care for this idea. If you're so fond of it, why don't you go?"

"Do you expect me to don your boots and hat as well?"

"Could you?" I give him a wry smile when he looks like he may take a swipe at me. Then, because his claws are too close to my face for comfort, I give in. "Fine. But if this plan of yours eventually lands me in the dungeons, I expect you to rescue me."

The cat settles on the wall, making himself comfortable. "No reason to be dramatic, Suzette. Go."

Again, I step into the light and wait my turn.

"Your business, mademoiselle?" A guard asks after his eyes rake over me.

Giving him a cool, indifferent smile, I say, "I have a gift for the king."

The guards open the doors for me. "His Majesty has made himself available for audiences with his people this afternoon. You may continue straight down the hall."

Pretending I'm far braver than I am, I stride into the cool entry. I hadn't expected to see the king himself. I had thought I would hand the rabbit off to a distant and aloof steward—like the man who met me in the hall before.

This time, I find myself waiting in a line in the throne room, listening to peasant's disputes. I try not to gawk at the finery, at the tapestries and the plush red runner. I keep my eyes trained on a small, floppy-eared dog who sits at the king's feet. When it's finally my turn, my heart races like a hummingbird's, and I feel as if I'm going to be sick.

"State your business," the king's head steward says from His Majesty's left-hand side.

I gulp and am careful to keep my face tilted down so my eyes are shadowed, as Puss instructed.

Pretend you're someone else. Pretend you're important.

"I have a brought a gift from my lady, the Marquise of Carabas," I say. It startles me how clear and confident my voice is.

When I dare a glance at the king, the first thing I notice is what a kind face he has. He wears a pleasant smile, which is quite a feat after the number of peasants' tiffs I listened to him sort through while I waited. That smile grows as he waves me forward. "I am not familiar with your lady. Where do you hail from?"

Where indeed?

"Far, Your Majesty."

He's opening his mouth, obviously wanting more of an answer, when a quiet murmur sounds from behind me. The king's eyes move to the room's entry, and, like a curious fool, I turn to follow them.

My knees go weak when I see Kerrick, and a shot of pain, sharp and hot, travels my veins. On his arm is the most beautiful girl I've ever seen. She's blond and ethereal, soft like a dove and her skin almost as pale. Her cheeks are flushed pink, and she looks up at Kerrick with the most adoring look.

I swallow, wishing I hadn't turned, wishing with all my being I'd stayed in Glenridge where I belong. As if I have no control over them, my eyes follow the pair as they make their way across the room and up the stairs until they're standing next to the king. Like a perfect gentleman, Kerrick offers the girl a seat on the empty throne at the king's side. Kerrick stands, his hand on the back of the throne and exchanges quiet, familiar greetings with the king.

My stomach knots and churns as my brain processes far too much information at once.

"My apologies, mademoiselle," the king says, returning his attention to me. "You were saying the marquise sends a gift?"

As I knew they would, Kerrick's eyes travel to mine. As soon as he sees me, he freezes, his shock mirroring my own.

CHAPTER 18

Once I rip my eyes from Kerrick, I somehow blunder through the rest of my audience with the king.

"Tell the Marquise that I am very pleased with her gift. What a fine hare. How is it your lady has come to know I have a fondness for poached rabbit?" The king hands the animal to his steward, who leaps forward to take the gift.

I give him a shrug that I hope is femininely mysterious, but I'm sure looks closer to seasick.

The moment His Majesty nods his dismissal, I rush from the hall. My throat's thick, and I'm too stunned to acknowledge the sting in my eyes.

I'm almost free of the castle when rushed footsteps sound from behind me. I glance about, almost frantic, wishing there were an audience so Kerrick would be forced to pretend indifference. Unfortunately, the hall is oddly empty.

"Suzette," Kerrick hisses.

He catches my hand the moment I turn and pushes through an ornate door that leads to another hall, pulling me with him. Without a word of explanation, he tugs me through a maze of corridors that I'll never find my way through should he suddenly abandon me.

Finally, when we're in an area that looks conspicuously like the servant's quarters, he stops.

"What was that about?" he demands.

His eyes are alight with confusion, and there's the slightest bit of frustrated anger in his gaze. His eyes travel to my new hat—the ridiculous thing that was supposed to hide my face and keep my identity under wraps, and he gives it an incredulous look.

He's too close, and I can't think. I yank my hand out of his.

"Fifth son of a minor lord?" I ask instead of answering his question. My voice drips with disdain.

Kerrick purses his lips, and a guilty look flashes across his face before it's replaced with irritation. "Your lady...the *Marquise?*"

I cross my arms. "It's none of your business, *Your Highness.*"

He flinches at the title.

We stare at each other, at an impasse. I won't tell him I'm here on a mission directed by my cat of all creatures, and he's already lied to me.

He's the prince.

The prince.

"I have to go." I turn from Kerrick, wondering if the stairs to our left will lead me down to an exit.

"Suzette."

With my back to him, I scrunch my nose and clench my eyes shut. It's only because he's so handsome, because he says my name with that soft catch at the end, that my pulse quickens. Any girl would find herself all aflutter. It's not because I, specifically, am hopeless and weak.

I look at Kerrick over my shoulder, simultaneously deciding, and informing myself, that I'm immune to his charms. "What?"

A tiny smile tips his lips, and he raises his eyebrows a fraction of an inch. "I like your hat."

Unbidden, my lips twitch. "I look like a bandit."

His mouth twists to the side as he thinks about my answer. Slowly, with maddening purpose, he takes in my outfit, making me want to fidget under his gaze. "More like a pirate."

At that, I hold out my hands, agreeing.

Then he frowns. "No that's wrong. You look like one of my father's guards...except far more lovely."

I bite back a smile and turn toward the stairs.

"When will I see you again?" he asks before I can run away.

"I'm no one." That crushing feeling of longing settles over me again. "And you're everything."

Kerrick shakes his head, wanting to argue with me but knowing that to protest my words would only be another lie.

"She adores you." I nod toward the last door we came through.

"She doesn't know me."

I manage a smile. "Don't concern yourself with that. She'll like you even more once she does."

He tilts his head, and soft frustration blends with amusement. "*Suzette.*"

"Enjoy the rabbit," I say, ignoring him.

"What are you plotting?"

"*I'm* not plotting anything." Hopefully, he misses the emphasis I place at the beginning of my response. "And I really do have to go. Are you going to show me a way out, or are you going to force me to wander the castle until I stumble on an exit?"

Kerrick steps nearer, smiling in a maddening way.

Neither of us moves closer, both knowing an invisible boundary has been drawn between us. Nothing is easy like it was in the meadow, where standing on my toes and kissing him would have been as natural as breathing.

"Are you going to marry her?" I ask, my voice quieter than I intend.

He lets out a long sigh and turns his head heavenward. "No. She's only one in a long line of prospects."

"Poor thing." I scoff under my breath. "It must be difficult being you."

"Sometimes."

I step away first and nod Kerrick toward the stairs. Though reluctant, he leads me down and out of the castle through a garden door. We exchange awkward, hesitant goodbyes.

"He likes partridges better than rabbits," he calls as I'm walking away.

Glancing back, I say, "Partridges?"

Kerrick crosses his arms. "They're his favorite."

Slowly, I nod. "Good to know."

***

PUSS KNEW. HE KNEW WHO KERRICK WAS FROM THE beginning. Yet he's as unapologetic as ever.

Supper is unusually quiet. My mind is on Kerrick, on the fact he not only lied to me but that there is truly no hope for a future with him now. If I'd known...well, he's right. I would have never agreed to spend time with him.

And no matter how Puss cajoles me, I won't go back. Whatever scheme he has in mind, it won't involve Kerrick or his father. I'll keep my distance. It's the only thing I can do.

Thomas and Eugene are quiet as well. I assume Thomas's mind is on his upcoming move, but I don't know why

Eugene broods. Finally, when I can't bear to be in my own head any longer, I ask him.

My eldest brother frowns and pushes his plate away, even though there is still meat left. "The harvest won't be enough."

Thomas looks at me, as startled by the news as I am. The field has done so well.

"The entire lot of it will be eaten up by the few necessary repairs that I must make to the mill if it will make it through another season. And next year will be the same. And every year after that. With only our small field, and with many of the local farmers building their own mills, we simply do not own enough to get ahead."

I'm not used to seeing my brother so melancholy, and it makes me nervous. I can't even disagree because I have no argument. He's right.

Thomas frowns. "I'll send money back—"

"No," Eugene says, cutting him off. "You'll need that money to get settled."

With nothing left to say, we fall quiet again. As soon as the dishes are cleared and cleaned, I escape to my corner of the loft. Without a word, Puss crawls on my lap and settles there, purring more to comfort me than because he's particularly content.

WHEN THE WHEAT IS TALL AND GOLDEN, AND THE STALKS SWAY in the breeze like waves in the ocean, Eugene and Thomas harvest the field. The grain now rests in large twined bundles, and we pray the rains will stay away until they dry. We're usually safe this time of year, but we still keep an eye on the youngest of the neighbor's cattle, watching for the signs of nervousness that Father swore meant bad weather is on its way.

I lean on an old fence and watch them now. A heifer grazes, and she looks as if she hasn't a care in the world. I glance from her to another young dairy cow, but they all have the same slightly glazed-over bovine look. With a sigh, I push away from the fence.

A welcome breeze blows from the north, taking some of the heat of the early autumn day with it. The days have been cooler, but today is hot. I push my hair back as I meander down the road toward the mill.

My basket is full to the brim with blackberries. Yesterday, when Puss and I were hunting, I noticed the bushes were heavy with the dark fruits. Early this morning, before I started on my daily chores, I slipped away to gather some before birds and bears stripped the bushes.

"Where's your cat?" a familiar voice calls from the lane behind me.

Smiling, I turn to greet Beau. "Good morning."

The chocolatier is properly pressed and perfect, and his light brown hair is light in the sun. He smiles with his whole face, and his enthusiasm is catching.

"You've been busy," he says, eying my basket.

"Help yourself." I offer the berries to him. As he takes several from the top, I ask, "What brings you away from your shop?"

"I requested a milk delivery from the Roslins." He motions toward our neighbor's cottage. "I'm running low."

"That's good, isn't it?" I ask as I start toward the mill. "Your shop is doing well?"

Beau falls into step next to me. "Well enough."

I give him a sideways glance. I'm fairly certain the shop is only a fleeting hobby, and he doesn't need the gold. Still, I hope if he's doing well he won't have the desire to move away.

We're nearing the cottage when the door swings open

and Baron Broussard steps from our humble home. I freeze, terrified to see the man on Eugene's land. But moments later, Eugene steps from behind him, smiling with what looks like relief.

Immediately, I pull Beau with me into a cluster of trees where we can watch the exchange without being seen.

"What's Broussard doing here?" Beau whispers.

My attention is fully on my brother, and I only shake my head to answer Beau's question.

Broussard is handsome for his age, which must be nearing his thirtieth year. His young wife passed away at the same time as my parents, all taken by the sickness that swept the village seemingly overnight. He has never remarried, and he has no heir. Though he owns half the village, he does not own the mill.

So what business does he have here?

After several more minutes of quiet discussion that I can't quite make out, the two men shake hands. Broussard mounts his horse and turns toward the lane, looking satisfied. The expression makes me uneasy, and I clench my basket tightly enough my knuckles turn white.

"If Broussard finds us hiding together in the brush, your reputation is sure to suffer," Beau whispers near my ear.

I nod, knowing he's right, and we step into the lane just before the baron rounds the bend.

Broussard smiles with recognition when he sees me, and he draws his horse to a halt. "Etta." His eyes travel over me, and a smile grows on his lips. "How grown up you've become."

That ill feeling grows. I dip in a curtsy. "Good day to you, Monsieur Broussard."

The man exchanges a few swift words of greeting with Beau, and then his attention returns to me. "I've heard you've become quite the huntress."

"Only adequate, I'm afraid." I shift, uncomfortable.

"Come hawking with me, Etta," he finally says. "It's a sport I'm sure you'll enjoy." As if he senses my reservations, he continues, "I won't take no for an answer."

I lower my eyes to the ground. "Thomas has taken his horse to Rynvale with him."

"You'll borrow one of mine." Then, with a farewell nod, he rides on. "I'll send the carriage to fetch you in the morning."

Beau whistles under his breath, and I turn to him. His expression is darker than usual, and I tap my finger against the basket as I wait for him to spit out whatever it is he wants to say.

"It's not every day a baron asks the miller's sister to go hawking," he finally says, more tactful than I expect.

I frown at the berries in my basket and continue toward the mill. Eugene spots me, but his smile dims when he sees Beau at my side.

"Monsieur Broussard just invited me to go hawking with him tomorrow," I tell Eugene, watching him closely to see if it's something he already knows.

Is this why the baron was here? Was he asking about me? Surely not.

Eugene's eyes go wide. Obviously, he's as surprised as I am.

"And what did you tell him?" my brother asks.

Unsure of myself, I glance at Beau and then look back. "I'm not in the position to decline an offer from a baron."

Beau looks uneasy, possibly more uneasy than my brother. "He didn't give you the chance to decline in any case."

Puss leaps from the side window of the mill. I know he's heard our conversation, and he doesn't appear to be impressed. Obviously, attention from Broussard is not what he had in mind when he spoke of grander things.

"Would you care to stay for tea, Monsieur Marchand?" Eugene asks, turning to Beau. "Sarah-Anne's here as well."

Though Eugene doesn't mention it, the cottage is too quiet with Thomas gone. We both feel his absence, and it's worse when Sarah-Anne visits Eugene. On those days, I'm very aware of how inconvenient my presence is.

I turn to Beau. "Yes, do."

"Please, call me Beau," he says to Eugene, and then he smiles at me. "And I'd be happy to."

Sarah-Anne greets us as we enter, and already I feel like a visitor in my own home. Her smile flickers when she sees Beau. Suddenly nervous, she busies herself with the tea.

It's the first time Beau's come inside the cottage, and my eyes dart this way and that, taking in the shabby interior. The only decorations are a dried wreath of herbs that hangs over the door to ward off insects and a faded and well-used quilt that rests on the chair in front of the hearth.

"Why did Broussard come calling?" I stir honey into my tea and then offer the small pot to Beau. He drizzles some in his cup, and I'm grateful that I took the time to harvest some from the hive I found in the forest last week. I may have returned that evening smelling like smoke and having been stung several times, but it's nice to have a little luxury to offer.

Sarah-Anne and Eugene exchange a look. They're obviously pleased with the news, but from their expressions I can tell that they don't think I will be.

"Well?" I prod.

Eugene lets out a long sigh and rests his arms on the table. "Monsieur Broussard has offered to buy the mill and let us live on as tenants."

I gape at him, not only shocked that my brother would

even consider the offer, but that he would look happy about it.

"Now before you say anything," Eugene says, leaning forward, "let me finish."

Crossing my arms, I snap my mouth shut.

"He said he will not charge us tenants' fees for the first three years, which will give us plenty of time to get back on our feet and buy the title back from him."

"But at what price?"

"Broussard only asks fifty percent of the profits we make from the mill."

"Fifty perfect!" I exclaim. My tea sloshes on the table as I scoot my chair back.

Knowing this would be my reaction, Eugene stays calm. "It's only fair when he'll let us live here for free."

I stand. "You live here for free now!"

Eugene stands and joins me on my side of the table. Clasping my shoulders, he says, "Etta, this harvest was good. Very good. But it's not enough to get us back on our feet."

"But I can…" I trail off. Catching a few spare rabbits here and there won't make up the difference that we need.

"Monsieur Broussard has offered us one hundred gold pieces—all of which I can put back into the mill. On top of that, I can buy a herd of cattle and chickens. Maybe even a few sheep." He glances at Sarah-Anne. "And I'll finally have enough that Sarah-Anne's father might give us his blessing."

I'm stunned by the sum, and I sink into my chair. One hundred gold pieces.

"He wouldn't make the offer if he didn't think he'd profit from it," Eugene says. "He expects to make his money back in that three years before I buy the land back from him. He wouldn't lend us the money if he didn't."

I shake my head. It's too risky. We have no way of

knowing how much Broussard will demand for the land at the end of the term.

"Etta..." Eugene's face softens, and his voice changes to sympathetic. "Sarah-Anne and I have already agreed. The mill is mine...this is not your decision to make."

He may as well strike me in the stomach. I suck in a quiet breath.

Sarah-Anne watches me with worried eyes, but I can't look at her.

"Very well," I say. Slowly, I sink back to my seat.

The rest of the hour passes with painful stretches of silence dotted with strained conversation. Just when I'm preparing to take Beau and flee, Eugene mentions the baron's hawking invitation to Sarah-Anne. Her eyes go wide at the news.

"You mustn't turn down an invitation from Broussard," Sarah-Anne says. "Especially when no one else has hinted at a possible courtship." Her eyes flit to Beau.

Beau wears a dry look on his face, her meaning not lost on him. As quickly as I can, I drain the rest of my tea and stand, yanking Beau up with me.

It's no surprise that the chocolatier seems somewhat relieved to be away. He thanks Sarah-Anne for her hospitality—in my home, no less, and then we're out the door. Puss joins us, and the three of us walk down the lane.

Comfortable with Beau at my side, I worry in silence.

Finally, it's Puss who speaks. "I don't care for Monsieur Broussard. No matter how I know you'll object, Suzette, it's time to take the king his partridges."

Beau nearly comes undone. Yelping, he jumps away from Puss, stumbles into a puddle in the middle of the road, and nearly falls on his hind end. Luckily he regains his balance. It would be a shame to ruin his fine coat.

Though I'm amused that the cat finally decided to give

someone else heart failure, I attempt to hide my smile for Beau's sake.

The chocolatier's eyes dart to me. "Tell me you heard that."

Instead of answering him, I look at Puss. "Did I scream that loudly at first?"

The cat tilts his head, obviously enjoying himself as well. "Yes."

Beau's gaze goes between me and Puss. His face has gone as pale as fleece. "How is this possible?"

Puss ignores the question and looks at me. "Do you still refuse to return to the castle?"

Crossing my arms, I nod.

"Very well." Puss turns to Beau although his words are still directed at me. "Then the boy will take the partridges for you."

Beau blinks, apparently affronted enough by this new bit to forgive the cat for speaking. "'Boy?' Excuse me, *cat*, but I am not—"

"Come along." Puss turns, not interested in whatever Beau was planning on saying, and heads toward the wheat field.

CHAPTER 19

Etta

"I DON'T QUITE UNDERSTAND WHAT IT IS I'M DOING HERE," Beau says as we lie on the far end of the newly-harvested field.

"It appears, to me at least, that you've decided to take orders from a cat," I answer.

"Yes," Beau whispers so as not to scare away the partridges that are finally coming near my bag. "But *why?*"

I rip my eyes from the trap. "You're here because I need you to deliver these partridges to the king for me." I wrinkle my nose. "Or rather, for the Marquise of Carabas."

Beau's eyes widen with what I swear is recognition followed by disbelief, but he quickly schools the expression. "Who?"

I give him an odd look and then say, "She's no one—not yet, but according to Puss, if we keep up with this ruse, I'll eventually assume her identity."

Beau raises a single eyebrow in question—a move he does spectacularly well. "How is the cat going to make you into a marquise? And where will he find you a march to lord over?"

I shrug; I have no idea where Puss intends to find me a

border land to belong to.

"And if you want to assume the title," he says, his smile turning slightly mischievous, "wouldn't it be easier to marry a marquis?"

"This is all trivial right now," Puss hisses. "For the time being, all you need to know is that Suzette must trap a brace of partridges, and you must take them to the king."

"Why me?" Beau asks.

"Because Suzette's heart is broken, and she cannot bear to face His Royal Highness." The cat's voice drips with disdain.

"No…" Beau groans quietly and rests his forehead on the ground. "Etta—please tell me it wasn't Prince Kerrick you were meeting in the woods."

I look away so he won't see how foolish I feel.

The chocolatier begins to rise. "I'm fairly certain I don't want to be part of this—"

"Get down!" Puss snarls.

Just when Beau opens his mouth to protest at being ordered around by the cat, two partridges stroll into my bag. I leap up and yank it closed. Without his usual words of criticism, Puss finishes the birds off for me.

"Now," Puss says to Beau. "You and I will go to Rynvale to see the king."

"And why would I do that?" Beau crosses his arms and sets his jaw at a stubborn angle.

Puss's tail twitches as it always does when he becomes agitated. "Because you don't like the idea of Broussard sniffing around Suzette any more than I do."

Grumbling under his breath, Beau yanks the bag from the ground.

"Why am I not coming?" I demand.

The cat turns to me. "Because it is already late, and we'll be forced to stay overnight. And, if I recall, you have a hawking engagement tomorrow morning."

Puss, apparently deciding our conversation is over, saunters toward Rynvale. I watch him go, irritated, and then I turn to Beau when the cat is out of earshot. "You don't have to do this."

Though he doesn't look happy, Beau places the bag over his shoulder and gives me a tight smile. "What are friends for?"

I try to smile back, but my mind is consumed with dread for tomorrow.

"Do you really think your fool of a cat knows what he's doing?" Beau asks.

"I hope so. There is no longer a place for me here, and, honestly, the way Broussard looked at me makes me uncomfortable."

Beau nods. "I'll find you as soon as I return."

"Your chocolate shop has been closed all day," I say. "If you go to Rynvale, it will be closed tomorrow as well. Will your business suffer?"

He waves my concern away. "A few days won't hurt anything."

Overwhelmed with gratitude, I step forward and wrap my arms around his middle, just like I would if Thomas or Eugene were doing me the great favor. "Thank you, Beau."

The embrace startles him so thoroughly; he goes as still as a statue. With my cheek pressed against his chest and my face hidden under my hair, I grimace. I've overstepped our boundaries.

As I pull away, he hesitantly pats my shoulder and steps back.

I try to smile, but now I just feel foolish.

Beau clears his throat and adjusts the bag. Then, after one more backward glance at me, he strides down the road after Puss.

CHAPTER 20

Beau

First, the cat can talk. Second, Etta smells like earth and sunshine.

Those two thoughts jumble about in my brain, making me dizzy. With Etta's bag over my shoulder, I stalk after the cat. Only after we've walked nearly fifteen minutes do I stop. I have a perfectly good horse. Why am I walking?

Growling under my breath, I continue on. There's no use going back now.

As if I'm trivial to his grand master plan, the cat doesn't talk again until we near Rynvale.

"Go straight to the king. Do not speak with the prince," the cat instructs just when I begin to worry that I've imagined the whole thing.

"Yes, Monsieur Cat."

His eyes flash with irritation at my tone, and I march past him and over the drawbridge. I eye the nobles who lounge around, hoping that I won't recognize anyone. Luckily, paying my respects to the king was the last thing on my mind when I settled in Glenridge.

Fortunately—or unfortunately, now that I think about it

—the king is in attendance. I wait my turn, more than ready to be done with all this. Finally, I'm admitted into the throne room. Next to His Majesty sits the man I remember from the street, the one who was speaking with Etta the first day I laid eyes on her. And it all shifts into place.

Steeling my jaw, it takes an amazing amount of restraint to keep from rolling my eyes. The prince looks like all the other princes I've ever met—including both of my second cousins on my mother's side. Kerrick's handsome. He's quick to smile and reeks of charm and charisma.

One made-to-order prince.

What really rankles is the lovely blond confection at his side. She's perfectly beautiful, probably smells like rose water and vanilla, and has eyes so large she looks far more innocent than she likely is.

The pair is too busy murmuring sweet nothings to each other to pay any attention to me. Any attention, that is, until I inform the king that I've come bearing a gift from the Marquise of Carabas.

At that, Kerrick's eyes whip to me so quickly, it's possible he's injured his neck. Some dark, petty part of me smiles at the thought.

"Partridges!" the king exclaims, and then he looks up, a wide smile on his face. "I really must meet your lady."

"She, as well, would love nothing more. Alas, the marquise has traveled overseas for a holiday, and we do not yet know when she will return. I will, however, promptly send a message, telling her how pleased you were with her gift." I bow, playing up my part as the marquise's devoted right-hand man, hoping to irk Kerrick. I'm not disappointed.

The cloak of easy charm has left the prince's face, and his features have gone sharp. He watches me with narrowed eyes, wondering just who I am and where I fit in.

"A shame," the king says, his voice full of sincere regret. "Where are you from, again? I can't quite remember."

"A march to the south of your kingdom."

The king nods and then leans forward. "Forgive me, but you must tell me, is this marquise of yours lovely?" He flashes a look at Kerrick. "Perhaps...unwed?"

Mangy cat—so that's his plan. But what does the Carabas family have to do with it?

"Yes, unwed. And may I answer you bluntly?" I ask.

The king nods, eager.

"She's the loveliest." I again glance at Kerrick, hoping to unsettle him. "Her hair is like spun gold, her eyes the fawn of a newborn doe. And her skin..." I let out an exaggerated sigh. "Perfection."

The prince has grown a satisfying color of red now that he realizes I'm speaking of Etta, a deep shade not unlike that of the poisonous tomato that merchants from the southeast try to pawn off on us in shipments.

King Deloge raises his eyebrows and clears his throat. "Well...splendid. Yes, quite. I hope you'll extend our invitation for a visit. I'd love nothing more than to meet her."

"I will, Your Majesty." I bow again and take my leave, pleased that I ruffled the prince's feathers but irritated now that I know what the cat is up to.

I leave quickly. Just as I'm out the doors, I locate the beast near the entrance, sitting on the garden wall to the left. Without a preamble, I pick him up by the scruff of the neck and stare him in the eye. "What does the family Carabas have to do with your schemes to marry Etta off to Kerrick?"

He hisses and twists to pull away. I watch him struggle for several gratifying moments and then drop him to his feet.

Indignant, he leaps back onto the wall so we're closer in height. "There's none in the Carabas family line left. They're gone, forgotten."

I meet his eyes, my face grim. "There's one."

Instead of answering, his whiskers twitch, and he studies me very carefully.

Using a great deal of self-control so that I don't give into the impulse to knock him off his high and mighty perch, I bow in front of the cat. "Allow me to formally introduce myself, feline. I am Beauregard Marchand Carabas...the Marquis of Carabas."

CHAPTER 21

Beau

THERE SHOULD BE NO SATISFACTION TO BE HAD FROM stunning a cat into silence. Sadly, I'm rather satisfied.

Finally, Puss stands, and with a calm, matter-of-fact tone, says, "You're not the marquis."

And with that, he hops from the wall and saunters through Rynvale. Again, I grab him, but, this time, I don't set him down no matter how he squirms. "I am."

Then, as if I have something to prove to this ridiculous beast, I show him my ring, hoping that if he knows something of the name, he'll at least recognize the crest. As soon as he sees it, he hisses.

I toss him to his feet.

He eyes me, his tail switching back and forth, highly agitated. "You could have stolen it."

Kneeling down, I say, "My father was the youngest son in the family line. The family title went to his eldest brother. Wishing them his best, Father left the family to make his fortune at sea. Which he did. He married a lovely noble-blooded adventuress—my mother—and lived a happy life...

at least he did up until a month before he died." I pause, making sure the cat is listening.

"Oh, please, Master Carabas," Puss drawls, irritated at this hiccup in his plans. "Do tell why the month was turbulent."

"Father received a letter from his youngest sister, apparently written on her deathbed, stating that the family estate was lost to an ogre of immense magic, and his brothers and parents, were dead."

"Tragic."

"It also said that he had inherited the title, the estate, the land, and all that goes with it."

The cat narrows his eyes, and for a moment I wonder if he's going to lunge at me. "How fortunate for you."

"But herein lies my problem. I can't seem to track down the ogre or the estate. And in all of the province, the only person—and I use that term loosely—who has any knowledge of my family name, is a cat." I tap Puss on the head, eliciting another hiss from him. "Why do you think that is?"

"Because they're under the ogre's curse," he growls, "and cats are immune."

I was beginning to figure as much.

"Do you know where my family's estate is located?" I ask.

He glares at me. "Yes."

"Excellent." I sit back on my heels. "I will make a deal with you. I'll help you with this charade if you'll take me to the castle. I have no desire to stay in this kingdom. As soon as I remove the ogre from my family home, I will be gone. Etta's free to live there, cost-free, for as long as she wants. Forever, if she wants."

I'd rather she do that than marry Kerrick.

"It's a start," the cat finally agrees. "But mark my words, young marquis, I intend for Etta to marry the prince."

Less satisfied, I stand. "Fine."

Though it's nearing evening, I decide to walk back to

Glenridge in the dark. We're almost out of Rynvale, just about to the stately gates, when the last person I had hoped to have a chat with finds me.

Unable to avoid the prince when I see him barrel through the crowd toward me, I stop, hoping to look only half as put out as I feel. "What a surprise. Hello, Your Highness."

"Who are you?" Kerrick demands without fussing over pleasantries. His eyes narrow at Puss. "And why do you have Suzette's cat?"

And it becomes apparent, to me at least, that I'll be staying the night in Rynvale after all.

CHAPTER 22

THE SUN HAS REACHED ITS HIGHEST POINT, AND NOW IT'S slowly lowering. I pace the lane in front of the mill. They should be back by now. I had hoped they would have been here when I returned from the baron's estate, but only Eugene was here to greet me.

My afternoon crawled by so slowly, I feel as if it's been days since Puss and Beau left for Rynvale, and not less than one. Hawking with the baron was uncomfortable, to say the least. He was overly attentive, overly complimentary, overly helpful. I've never been so relieved to be away from a man in my life. And the whole time, he just kept smiling in an indulgent way that made me slightly queasy. I'm sure nearly every other girl in the village would be grateful for his attention, but the whole ordeal made me wish I'd stayed hidden in the brush with Beau yesterday.

"Etta," Eugene calls from the field. "Can you spare a moment from your pacing to help me?"

Sighing, I turn from the road. I spend the rest of the afternoon helping Eugene thresh wheat. By evening, I begin to grow nervous. Where are they?

"Can you manage supper for yourself tonight?" I ask my brother as I pull a shawl from my peg by the door. My arms ache from the day's chore.

Eugene glances out the window. "Where are you going this late?"

"To the village. I need to see Beau."

My brother frowns. "Etta, I'm not sure it's wise—"

A knock sounds at the door, saving me from cutting Eugene off myself. I open it, hoping for Beau and Puss, but only Sarah-Anne stands on the other side.

My face falls.

"Happy to see you as well, Etta," Sarah-Anne says with a laugh as she brushes past me.

Eugene lights up when he sees her, and, if nothing else, he won't mind me leaving now. I wave a quick goodbye and dart into the evening. The sun is just setting, so I'll have plenty of light for the walk to Glenridge. I reach the chocolate shop just as the lampposts are being lit for the night. Unfortunately, I find the windows dark, and the door is locked.

With a worried sigh, I lean my back against the wood and close my eyes.

"Etta?" someone calls from down the street.

My eyes fly open. There, not far away, Beau and Puss make their way toward me. I let out a relieved breath, and then I set my hands on my hips. When the pair is near, I demand, "What could have taken you this long?"

A perturbed look crosses Beau's face. "Everything was well and fine in Rynvale until your *beloved* took me aside and interrogated me on your whereabouts. He detained me until late this afternoon."

My chest tightens at the mention of Kerrick. Part of me had hoped he wouldn't be in attendance when Beau saw the king. Another part was hoping that something just like this would occur.

"What did he say?" I ask, trying to appear only mildly curious, but my voice is too eager.

"Well," Beau begins, "at first he was *very* interested to know who I was." Beau can't quite hide his smirk, but he does his best to school the expression when I give him a chastising look. "Don't look at me like that. I set his mind at ease, explaining that your heart is nothing but true to him."

I grimace. "You said that?"

"Something to that effect." He shrugs. "I can't remember the specifics."

For a moment, I study Beau and wonder what Kerrick's reaction to him was. If the prince were inclined to jealousy, Beau would likely make him see green. Though, in the most traditional sense, Beau's not as handsome as Kerrick, there is a reason all the girls in Glenridge swoon over the chocolatier.

Beau crosses his arms and cocks his head. "What?"

Blinking, disconcerted, I look away. "Did he say anything about me?"

Looking uncomfortable, Beau furrows his brow. He says, his voice deadpan, "Only that the days are endless now that you're gone from his life, and he's desperate to see you again."

My heart warms at the thought of it, but the warmth is quickly replaced with an ache. Why did I send Beau in my place? Kerrick could have told me those things himself.

Still, I'm uneasy about all of this now that Kerrick's involved.

Beau unlocks the door and ushers us inside. As always, the smell of chocolate overwhelms me, making me hungry and reminding me I skipped supper.

"You're missing the point," Puss says to me, unable to stay silent any longer, "which would be that the king was very pleased with the partridges you sent."

"You mean that *you* sent," I say.

Puss tilts his head, silently informing me that we're not going to squabble over details.

After Beau lights several candles, he starts a fire. The evening is not quite chilly enough for one to be needed, but the cozy crackle is welcoming. Puss, unable to help himself, settles on the rug and stretches in front of the warm flames.

"How was hawking?" Beau sits at the table.

I take the seat opposite him. "Awkward."

"Do you think it was simply a nice gesture…or was there more purpose there?"

Rolling my shoulders, I turn my gaze toward the fire. "If I were anything other than the miller's sister, I would say there appears to be a purpose." I turn back to Beau. "But I *am* the miller's sister. It's an absurd thought."

Beau studies me like my brothers did not so long ago. "Perhaps, but you are very lovely."

For some reason, when he says it, I can't help but smile. "Not lovely enough to become the baroness."

Leaning forward, his eyes suddenly serious, Beau says, "Lovely enough to enchant a prince."

Uncomfortable, I turn my eyes down and study the signet ring he wears. "Did the king ask again where you were from?"

Slowly, Beau nods.

"The boy told him his lady hailed from a march far to the south," Puss says before Beau can answer. There's a glint in Puss's eyes as he turns his gaze on Beau. He doesn't seem impressed with the chocolatier's impromptu ad-libbing.

Beau shrugs. "It sounded plausible."

"What good will deceiving the king do?" I ask Puss. "Even if he eventually sees me and believes that I'm this fine lady, I will have nothing to show for it—no land, no riches. I fail to see how any of this is helpful."

"Patience," Puss says, continuing to be cryptic in his responses. He yawns wide, and then, as if deciding it's a good time for a nap, closes his eyes and stretches onto his side.

I shake my head and turn my attention back to Beau. "Thank you, all the same."

"Do you love him?" Beau asks. Though curious, he looks indifferent to my response. "Kerrick?"

"I like him a great deal." I rub the spot above my collarbone that begins to ache every time I think about the prince. For the first time, feeling like I truly have a friend in Beau, I admit, "I think some part of me might."

Frowning, Beau says, "Even though he lied to you?"

Slowly, I nod. "I can forgive him. Besides, it's not worse than whatever it is I'm doing to his father."

Beau looks at the cat, who is now asleep. "Puss intends you to marry the prince—that's his plan."

My heart nearly seizes in my chest. "That's not possible."

"It's very possible for a prince to marry a marquise." Beau swallows, looking as if he's deciding something. "I'll help you however I can."

"You'd do that?" I ask, elation churning with my doubts. "You'd do that for me?"

His jaw tightens as he smiles. "Well...we're friends, aren't we?"

I want to clasp my hands over his, but I remember how tense he became when I embraced him, so I keep them to myself. "Yes."

He claps his hands on the table as he stands, the conversation obviously closed for now. "I'm starving. Let's find something to eat."

CHAPTER 23

"YOU'RE A NATURAL," BROUSSARD SAYS AS HE MATCHES my pace.

It's my second outing with the baron, and I'm not any more comfortable with him than I was the first time. He's handsome enough, charming as well, but I can't help but think he's intentionally swindling my brother.

I do enjoy the horses, however, and it's nice to be riding through the fields and meadows outside Glenridge instead of lying stomach-down in them.

As we attempt to flush the hares out, Broussard's hawk perches in a tree, waiting.

"Rumors are abounding through the village that you've become a proficient huntress."

I glance at my companion for the afternoon. Perhaps most would warm at his praise, but his words make me uncomfortable. "I do well enough."

Broussard glances over. "There are other rumors of you as well."

Purposely avoiding his gaze, I scan the field, staying silent.

"Is there any truth to them?" he asks. "What are your feelings for the chocolatier?"

"May I be blunt, Monsieur?"

He smiles. "Of course."

I meet his eyes and give him a bare smile. "I don't think that's any of your business."

The baron tips his head back and laughs. "Fair enough."

We ride through a thick patch of brush, and a rabbit darts from the bracken. Immediately, the hawk cries out and swoops down to snare her prey. It's an impressive thing, watching the hawk hunt.

Broussard, delighted, dismounts his horse and offers the bird a strip of raw meat in trade for the hare. He holds the animal up for me to inspect.

"It's a fine rabbit," I say.

He nods, pleased. "Not many women would have the stomach for this sport."

So that's what he likes about me. I suppose it's flattering, in a way, that he admires what others have begun to gossip about.

We ride the rest of the afternoon, and the hawk takes out several more hares. It's nearing the golden hours of the evening when we ride back to the cottage. Eugene is either in the mill or the woods, and our land is quiet and still.

Broussard offers his hand, helping me from my horse. "You are not happy with the agreement your brother and I have made."

His words take me by surprise, and I have no time to hide the look on my face. He laughs, reading me easily. "What if I were to burn the contract and let him keep the gold I loaned him?"

"Why would you do that?" I ask, but I already know.

"I'm fond of you, Etta, and I've been lonely these last few years." He looks over the hill, toward his estate. "You are fine and young, and I think we have enough in common that we could be very content."

Content.

I don't want to be content. I want to be wildly happy, desperately in love.

"And if I decline?" I ask, my voice quiet.

The baron gives me a tight smile. "I'm a man of business."

It's not a threat, not exactly. More of a statement, something I already know.

Nodding, I look toward the field. "Thank you for today."

"Think about my offer, Etta."

I smile, but it's only for appearances. Inside, it feels as if an ulcer burns at my stomach. The baron rides down the lane, walking the horse I just rode on a lead beside him.

Broussard's offer would make a world of difference for my family. Eugene would never again have to worry about the mill. Thomas could pursue his whittling—do what he loves instead of working for the carpenter in Rynvale. And I would be taken care of—I'd never eat pottage again, never wear patched-together rags.

I'd live the rest of my life here, in Glenridge. Somehow, it just doesn't seem like enough anymore.

"Good evening, Etta!"

I turn toward the lane, and a genuine smile tugs at my lips when I see Beau riding toward me on his chestnut mare, just back from another audience with King Deloge.

"How was it?" I ask as he dismounts.

He sets his horse free to graze in our overgrown pasture and removes his riding gloves. "Utter pandemonium. I waited over an hour for a two-minute audience." Beau sees my expression and smiles. "But the king was very pleased with your quails."

"That's something, at least."

Studying me, Beau crosses his arms. "I passed Broussard on the way here."

"He just left." I think back to the conversation and frown. "He very subtly asked me to marry him."

Beau's eyebrows shoot up. "Already?"

I shrug. "He says that he'll burn the contract he made with Eugene if I say yes, let my brother keep the gold to invest in the mill."

"What was your answer?" His expression is suddenly serious.

"I didn't answer." I watch the sun sink lower, toward the mountains. "Would it be very selfish of me to say no to him?" I look back at Beau. "When my saying yes would make such a difference in the quality of my brothers' lives?"

"There are other options, Etta." Beau crosses his arms. "If things go as Puss has planned—"

"He's a cat." I feel helpless. "The whole thing is folly."

Beau steps in front of me, lifts his hands like he's going to take my shoulders, and then changes his mind and drops them to his side. "I said I would help you, and I will. No matter if this scheme works with Kerrick or not."

There's something about Beau, a genuineness I've come to truly appreciate. But there's something else now. I study him, wondering what it is. His moss-green eyes have light flecks of amber that I've never noticed, probably because we've never stood this close before. His lips are more angular than Kerrick's, not as full.

"Don't marry Broussard," he says, his voice quieter than before.

His eyes search mine, and I go still.

"Do you know you smell like chocolate?" I whisper after several moments. A smile tugs teasingly at my lips, and I purse them to keep from laughing.

Beau's gaze drops to the ground, and his cheeks grow a

shade darker. He rubs the back of his neck as he bites back an embarrassed grin, and he takes a step away.

Laughing, I nudge his shoulder. "No wonder all these poor village girls are besotted with you when you smell like that."

Raising an eyebrow, cheeks still red, Beau meets my eyes. His tone suddenly very serious, he says, "Not all of them."

Another moment passes between us, but this one takes me by surprise. I begin to question something I know as fact —and that is that Beau is not interested in the village girls.

And I am most certainly a village girl.

I've looked at him for a moment too long, and he raises an eyebrow, waiting for me to respond. Gulping, I turn from him and laugh the sentiment away as if it were a joke. Pretend something didn't just resonate in my core.

"I should go…" he says.

I meet his eyes. "Thank you for going to the king."

He nods and turns to leave; then he stops and looks over his shoulder. "You owe me a ride. Come out with me tomorrow."

"Tomorrow?" My mouth goes dry. "You realize I still don't have a horse."

"I'll borrow one from the Roslins," he says, speaking of the family who lives at the next farm over, the ones who provide milk for his shop.

I begin to shake my head. "I don't think—"

Beau cocks his head to the side and pins me with his gaze. "Come on. Don't turn me down twice."

Setting my hands on my hips, I say, "You're as stubborn as Puss."

With a grin and a wave, he calls over his shoulders, "I'll meet you here in the morning."

CHAPTER 24

Beau

"WHERE'S THE MOST EXOTIC PLACE YOU'VE TRAVELED?" ETTA asks as we ride through the countryside with no real destination in mind.

I think of her question, and hundreds of locations pass through my memory—deserted beaches, black forests, scorching deserts. "Vionella is rather exotic," I finally answer. "It's where my mother currently lives. I have a small cocoa plantation there, and I'm hoping to expand soon."

Her smile is tempered with an emotion I can't read, but she smiles. "Tell me about it."

"The weather's temperate—there are no true seasons. We have a small estate on a cliff that borders the sea, and it always smells of summer."

And I'll never go back without remembering Etta and the way, she too, smells of sunshine.

"It sounds lovely," she says.

"Perhaps I'll show it to you someday." I say the words without thinking, and then I wince. In what world will I have the chance to take Etta across the sea? Certainly not the one where she's in love with Kerrick.

Again, she smiles that odd sort of smile and then changes the subject to Thomas, who visited them a few days ago for the first time since he took on his apprenticeship.

Puss darts ahead of us, into a bush. We're traveling at a sedate, leisurely pace, and he tired of sitting on Etta's lap early in the afternoon.

The day is clear, perfect for a ride. The autumn countryside has faded to shades of gold and olive, but all except a few leaves on the trees are green. Late flowers bloom in the fields, brightly colored daisies that like the warmth of the day but thrive in cool evenings.

"Do you miss him?" Etta asks when I think the conversation is over.

I turn to her, raising my brows in question.

"Your father." She shrugs in apology and looks forward. "I'm sorry. You don't have to answer that."

"I do miss him." As seems to be a habit, I rub my signet ring through the leather of my riding glove. "Sometimes it's surreal that he's gone and not just at sea."

"Did you sail together?"

I nod. "Many times, but in the last few years, I'd taken command of my own ship, gone my own way. Cocoa was not his shipment of choice."

"Do you love it? The sea?"

Turning to her, I smile. "I do."

"And you miss it too?" Her eyes search mine, and I'm not sure what she's hoping to find there. Softly, she continues, "I suppose I'm asking if you're unhappy here."

I hold her gaze a moment longer, long enough that she begins to fidget with the reins of her horse. "No, I'm not unhappy. Do I miss the sea? Yes, almost more than anything. But right now, this is the only place I want to be."

Her smile is quick, and it does funny things to my pulse. "I'm going to talk with Broussard this evening."

The abrupt change in conversation is enough to give a man whiplash. "Oh?"

"I'm going to decline his offer."

"I promise things will work out." I say it as the vow it is.

Etta smiles, biting her lip, and nudges her borrowed mare forward. "I believe you."

CHAPTER 25

THE HOT DAYS OF SUMMER ARE GONE, THOUGH THE afternoons are still pleasantly warm. It rained last night, but today is clear. Geese are just beginning their winter migrations, and flocks can be seen high overhead. As soon as they appeared, Puss was eager to bag one. But they are more suspicious than the animals native to our province and are too large to trap.

Though I was squeamish at first, I've shot several with my crossbow. The geese fetch a fine price at the butcher's shop, and Beau assured me the king was impressed as well.

The chocolatier has taken several trips into Rynvale, carrying gifts from the marquise to the king. Each time he returns, I hope for a message from Kerrick, but Beau hasn't spoken to the prince since that first day.

According to Puss, the geese are not grand enough. We need something larger.

And that larger something ends up being the young stag we're watching now. As the deer grazes, his ears twitch this way and that, but, so far, he doesn't seem to sense our presence.

"Let's hunt more geese," I whisper to Puss.

Shooting birds is one thing. This is completely different. I feel ill just thinking of it. The weight of my crossbow grows heavier each minute we linger in the brush.

The cat twitches his whiskers. "No."

"How do you expect me to drag it back to Glenridge?" I demand.

The cat shifts, irritated I won't be quiet. "Beau said he'd meet us this morning. He'll take care of it."

I purse my lips, wondering if I'll get lucky and the stag will dart away. Out of excuses, I raise my bow.

Still, the stag stands, oblivious.

I draw a deep breath, and as I let it out, I shoot the arrow. It meets its target, but instead of falling as the geese do, the deer darts.

"No!" I cry as it takes off.

"After it!" Puss has already leaped to his feet. "I'll go back for Beau, and we'll find you. Do not lose it!"

I race through the forest, stumbling through bushes and tripping over logs, attempting to track the animal. The forest trails have turned to mud with the rain, and I trip, falling face-first into the muck. Ignoring the sticky glop, I push myself to my feet and keep after the stag. Finally, he stops, near death. Hidden behind a large bush, I rest my hands on my thighs and draw in silent gasps of air, grimacing when I examine the damage. The mud is already drying in my braid and along my face and arms, but it's still wet and thick on my clothes.

I scratched my arm when I fell, and blood drips from the wound. A spot near my hairline stings, and I find blood there as well. Sighing, I brush dead leaves and bits of twig off my soiled shirt and wait for the deer to either succumb to death or take off again.

Just when I think it's about to fall, a noise behind us

spooks him. I leap, just as startled as the stag. The creature doesn't make it far this time. He staggers two steps, and then he finally collapses.

Beau stands behind me on horseback, and his eyes go wide when he takes in my less-than-tidy appearance. "What happened to you?"

A sharp remark is on the tip of my tongue, but I hold it back. I must look like I'm about to snarl, however, because Beau raises his eyebrows and bites back an amused grin.

"Good, Etta," Puss says as he looks at the fallen stag.

I frown at the cat and wave my hand toward my kill. "What now?"

"It must be dressed." Beau swings down from his horse and offers me the sharp, long dagger from his sheath.

Shaking my head emphatically, I step back. "Absolutely not. I'm not doing that."

When I expect Puss to argue, he only cocks his head, listening to some unheard noise in the forest. His mind works behind his sharp eyes, but he doesn't share his thoughts with us. Finally, he says, "Beau will dress the deer."

Beau looks like he wants to argue the command, but he only nods.

"Etta," Puss continues. "There is a shallow spot in the creek not far from here. I'll take you there, and you can wash yourself off."

My face is tight with splotches of dried mud, and I rub some of the dirt off my cheek. "I'm fine."

The cat stares at me, his green eyes intent. "You are to pose as a marquise, Etta. You can't wander about looking like a troll." When I begin to argue, he lets out a feline version of a sigh. "If you do this one small thing, your fortune will be made."

I very much doubt that, but I finally agree.

The spot Puss speaks of is a little too near the road for my comfort, but the cat assures me I'll be well hidden by the thick brush growing at the edge of the bank.

"Keep watch," I command as I pull my mud-crusted clothes off. For modesty's sake, I plunge into the cold, clear water as quickly as possible.

I scrub my shirt and breeches first, wring them out, and lay them on a rock on the bank to dry. Then I sink back in the creek and begin to wash the dirt from my hair. After several moments, the chill of the water isn't as sharp. I close my eyes and lean my head back. Above me, birds sing, and the warm autumn sun shines through the dappled canopy.

My peace is quickly shattered by Beau shouting my name, sounding almost panicked. I sit up immediately and reach for my clothes.

They're gone.

Thrashing in the water, I whirl about, looking for my shirt and breeches.

"They were right here!" I exclaim, flustered as I hear his voice draw nearer.

"Etta!" Beau yells. "Where are you?"

"Beau, I'm here!"

I'm just about to tell him to stay put—that I'm fine—when Puss shouts from nearby, "A carriage approaches. Run to them, Beau! Tell them the marquise has been robbed, and they will be bound to help."

"Where is she?" Beau demands.

"GO!" the cat roars.

My heart nearly stops, and I sink further into the creek, hoping to hide myself. What is the wretched beast up to now?

As soon as I hear Beau rush through the brush far to my right, Puss pokes his head through the grass on the bank. Urgently, he says, "When they arrive, you will say you are the Marquise of Carabas. Do you understand?"

"What have you done with my clothes?" I demand.

"They are the least of your worries." He glances back, toward the road, where Beau yells for a carriage to stop. "If you mess this up, Etta, we will not have another chance. When they find you, you will pretend to be overcome. You were robbed, do you understand? The villains took off with your lady's maid, and they stole your fine clothes."

With those words, he again darts into the grass.

"Cat," I hiss. "Puss!"

The cat does not come back.

Footsteps crash through the nearby brush. I don't have long until they find me.

"She's here somewhere," Beau says, his voice strained with worry. "She screamed for me, but I ran to you for help as soon as I heard you approaching."

I swim to the shadows and hide behind a boulder at the edge of the bank. Several men appear over the hill.

"I'm here," I croak. Despite the freezing water, my face burns.

When I get my hands on that cat, I'm going to roast him and have a muff made from his fur.

Beau spots me first, and his eyes widen with shock. Though I'm mostly hidden, he immediately looks at his feet. "Et—" he begins, and then he chances a glance at the guards he's brought with him. "...*My lady*, are you injured?"

Beau's not going to be pleased when he finds out that Puss tricked him.

"My clothes were stolen." My voice is weak from humiliation, and I gulp a breath. "And the bandits have taken my lady's maid."

At my words, half the group darts back to the road to track down the villains. Just as I finish the rest of what Puss instructed me to say, another man breaks through the brush to join the group.

I nearly die right here in the creek.

Kerrick's mouth works, but he finds no words. The prince looks even more gallant than usual with the sun streaming down on his light hair. His gaze searches mine, bewildered, confused...and perhaps a little overwhelmed to find me without my clothes. With wide eyes, he immediately turns to Beau for help.

The chocolatier must now realize the cat duped us both, and he wears a look that is less than amused. He angles toward Kerrick and extends a hand toward me. "Your Highness, please allow me to introduce my lady, the illustrious Marquise of Carabas."

CHAPTER 26

Beau

KERRICK LOOKS AT ME FOR HELP. AS IF I HAVE THE ANSWERS.

You're the prince. Figure it out for yourself.

Etta's mortified, my pulse is racing, and Kerrick looks about as helpful as the boulder Etta's hiding behind.

Shaking my head, keeping an eye out for that cat, I ask, "Do you have a blanket the marquise could wrap herself in?"

One of the king's men, the one who can't seem to tear his eyes away from Etta's face and dripping wet hair—because that's all we can see of her—stammers something unintelligible.

"Anything?" I prod, starting to lose my patience with the lot of them.

Not that I had much of it to begin with, not after Puss told me Etta had been attacked and then wouldn't tell me where she was. He was just "run to the carriage, Beau" and "hurry, Beau, if you tell them she's the marquise they'll help her."

And what did I do? I blindly listened. *Idiot.*

Etta shivers behind her rock, but if it's from the stress of the situation or the cold water, I don't know. Probably both.

Grumbling under my breath, I turn toward the road. "I'll find something."

Reluctant to leave Etta on her own, I glance over my shoulder. She meets my eyes and purses her lips. A silent agreement passes between us. It goes something like, "we should drown Puss in the creek."

My lips turn up in a grim smile, and Etta, despite the predicament and the scratch on her head that is still persistently oozing blood, almost smiles back.

But not with the starry-eyed wonder she reserves for her prince.

I thought I was going to have to wade in the creek after Etta the moment she laid eyes on Kerrick. Her face went white, and she practically hyperventilated on the spot. A sad and embarrassing death it would be to die in three feet of water.

And something tells me I'd likely inherit her cat.

"Is she...?" the king asks, leaning out of the carriage when he sees me coming for it. He looks genuinely concerned, and I feel guilty for having deceived him, even if it wasn't exactly my fault.

"Fine, Your Majesty," I answer. "Do you have a blanket to spare?"

Immediately, a small figure leaps to her feet from the other side of the king. I hadn't noticed her before, but I instantly recognize her now. It's the blond princess from the palace, the one whose dresses look like they are designed by a pastry chef and appears as if she should smell like a rose garden. She's in some sort of pink gauzy material today, covered in ruffle after ruffle of the stuff.

"Please, take this," she says, offering me a lap blanket. Her violet eyes—*truly, violet*—are earnest with the desire to be helpful.

Doubtful, I accept the tiny blanket, which will only cover the most important—

I stop the thought there, my ears already growing warm. Etta will murder me if I show up with this.

"Do you think there's something a bit more...concealing?" I ask. "The...er...bandits have stolen her clothes."

The king looks properly horrified, and, once again, I delight in the thought of dunking Puss in the creek.

"She's quite all right," I assure him. Then I realize I left her bleeding. "Except for a few bumps and scratches. Well, and right now she's cowering behind a rock in the creek for modesty's sake."

Standing, the king takes off his long, red robe and hands it to me. "Then what are you standing here for? She'll catch her death."

I need no further prodding. I accept the robe and run back the way I came, through the weeds, bushes, and reeds.

By the time I return, Kerrick has resorted to attempting small talk, the simpleton.

"Fine weather, isn't it?" I just hear him say as I arrive. "I thought with the rain last night it would be a dreary day."

Etta's running her hands down her dripping hair. She's trying to smooth the water out of it, I suppose, as she gives him an incredulous look. Well, mostly incredulous. She also looks slightly besotted.

But when she sees me carrying a cover-up, I have all her attention. Relief softens her features.

At the same time, we both realize that I have to get it to her somehow.

But how?

Without asking her opinion on the matter, I leap to a rock in the middle of the creek and then jump to the other side.

"Beau," she hisses as I draw near, even though I'm not looking in her direction.

Once on the other side, I stretch my arm out behind me, reaching as far as I can with the cloak in my hand.

"Turn around," Kerrick instructs his men. It's the first wise thing he's said since he arrived. "Everyone back to the carriage."

The men retreat, and I hear Etta stand—try not to listen to the water as it drips back to the creek. I clench my eyes shut, even though I'm not facing her, and fight a slightly wicked thought that makes me much less of a gentleman. But what man wouldn't at least *think* it?

Then I realize that Kerrick is likely *thinking* it as well, and my shoulders go rigid.

Darting like the deer she just chased down, oblivious to my thoughts or Kerrick's, Etta grabs the cloak and leaps to my side of the bank.

"Are you decent now?" I whisper.

"Yes."

I turn and can't help but smile. The cloak is far too long for her. It pools on the ground, and the bottom hem partially dips into the water. Her hair lays plastered to her head, she trembles slightly, and her cheeks are bright pink.

Etta bites her lip, self-conscious. Keeping her voice low, she asks, "Have you seen Puss?"

"No." I rip a strip from my undershirt and press the material against the scratch on her head. "He's wisely making himself scarce."

"May I turn?" Kerrick calls from the other side. He's the only one left.

Etta gives me an uncertain look and holds the strip in place so I can move my hand. "All right."

Kerrick turns slowly, and then he lets out a sigh when he sees her. Swiftly, he jumps over the creek, taking a slightly shallower, easier route than I did.

Wouldn't want to get his boots wet, after all.

And then Etta's in his arms, and I'm feeling particularly uncomfortable.

"Etta," he murmurs as he holds her. "What happened?"

I expect her to sink against him, tell him what a trying experience this has been—it would be no lie. But, instead, and much to my surprise, her eyes slide to me. And not in a way that tells me she wants me to leave, but, rather, in a way that begs for rescuing.

But from the explanation or the prince? I'd rather it be the latter, but I'm sure it's the first.

Let's see what I can come up with.

"We were riding," I begin, and then I nod, liking the direction this is headed. "And Etta's horse spoo—"

Kerrick gives me a wry look. "Don't pretend this wasn't staged." He turns his eyes on Etta. "It was brilliant, but perhaps a little risqué."

She gulps. "I assure you, I had nothing to do with it."

Slowly, Kerrick turns accusing eyes on me.

I hold my hands up. "No, no. Not my idea either."

"A third player in this ruse?" the prince asks. "Have I met this person?"

And this is the moment Puss decides to join us. He saunters through the grass, only looking as innocent as any cat can look on any given occasion—not very.

For half a moment, I wonder if the cat will declare himself. I wait for him, wondering if he'll decide to. But, apparently, he doesn't deem Kerrick worthy. Part of me—a ridiculous part—takes a sick measure of pride in that.

That's right, Your Highness, this here barn cat holds me in higher esteem than you. How do you like that?

Pathetic.

"It doesn't matter," Etta says with a sigh. "I'm cold and wet, and I just want to go home."

"How will that work?" I ask. "Are you going to have His Majesty drop you off at the mill?"

A line forms between Kerrick's brows as he thinks. "Tell me the story you've concocted, and I'll take care of the rest."

Etta turns to him, smiling radiantly. Apparently one of us is comfortable leaving her fate in the prince's hands.

It certainly isn't me.

CHAPTER 27

THE KING'S CARRIAGE IS FAR MORE OPULENT THAN THE ONE Monsieur Broussard sent for me, and, at the time, that had been the nicest thing I'd ever ridden in. The interior is plush, the fabric red, and every bit of trim is gilt with gold.

The king sits opposite me with Kerrick to his right. A girl who's been introduced as Princess Sabine of Bethshire perches on the prince's other side, and a white dog sits on her lap. All three wear a smile, and all are of differing temperatures. The king is warm and cordial, Kerrick's is cool and nervous, and Sabine's is filled with worry.

From the moment I was swept into the carriage, with my dripping hair and shaking shoulders, the princess has fretted over me like a mother hen—even though I'm fairly sure I'm older than she is by a year, possibly two. Her hands are clasped in her lap, and her mouth is turned down in a sympathetic pout. Whenever I accidentally meet her eyes, her expression turns falsely bright, as if she's attempting to bolster my spirits.

And that's how she's looking at me right now. I attempt to smile back and then turn to look past Beau, who's on my left, to gaze out the window. They've closed the drapes on my side, all fussing that I'll catch my death if I'm subjected to the slightest breeze.

How delicate we nobles are.

Fields go by, and, slowly, we draw closer to Rynvale. His Majesty insisted I allow them to escort me back to the castle, and he urged me to stay for several days, so I may give myself time to recover before I consider traveling again. That, and he'd like me to wait until his men track down the culprits.

I swallow, feeling more than a little guilty over that. King Deloge has six guards scouring the countryside, looking for bandits and one kidnapped lady's maid—all who don't exist.

The king is now under the impression, thanks to Beau, who came up with a quick story to feed to Kerrick, that I was bucked from my horse while out on a pleasure ride and fell fully into a mud puddle. With my delicate nature, there was no way I could consider traveling all the way back to my estate soiled in that way, so I took my lady's maid and bathed in the nearby creek. It's at that time the bandits sneaked upon us, stole my fine, jewel-encrusted gown, and took off with my maid.

Such a mercy that the king should, chance of all chances, happen by at that exact moment, saving me. As I glance at the cat sleeping peacefully on my lap, who's ignoring Sabine's gleeful, vibrating dog, I wonder if anyone would think it odd if I were to toss him from the moving carriage.

In an attempt to lighten the mood, Sabine asks the king a question about the herring from the supper they shared last night. As he and Kerrick laugh with her about it, I sneak a peek at Beau.

He's my steward, Kerrick explained to the king—as close to the marquise as a brother and always at her side, Beau had added to Kerrick's chagrin. For which Kerrick replied in an unusually wry tone, "Except when you're delivering gifts to my father."

Beau only smiled.

My faux steward meets my gaze now, his light green eyes bright with the secret shared between us. And the strangest thing happens. My heart, which is fully focused on Kerrick, skips a single, solitary beat before its pace returns to normal.

Beau lifts an eyebrow, a perfected move unique to him, questioning the odd look on my face.

Quickly, I adjust my expression and subtly shake my head. Then I look past him, again trying to focus on the fields and cottages that go by.

CHAPTER 28

Beau

IN THE BEGINNING, I WAS INTRIGUED BY ETTA. ENCHANTED even. But I'm alarmingly taken with her now. It's undeniable at this point. Being around her more this last month, getting to know her—it's taken its toll on me.

But who knows how long it will last? A month? Two? It's September now. I can't imagine this...infatuation...will linger past November.

That should be long enough to oust the ogre from my family home, get Etta settled there—as far from Kerrick and Monsieur Broussard as possible, and be about my business yet again.

The tropical port of Vionella is lovely in the winter, and I haven't seen Mother for almost half a year. Perhaps I'll buy more land for cocoa trees. It's a good business, one Father scoffed at to begin with. But now I have eleven chocolate shops, including the one in Glenridge, scattered throughout the kingdoms, and business is good. The nobility can't seem to get enough of the rich, exotic drink from overseas, and I'm happy to supply it. It's a win/win situation for us all.

After I train someone to take over my position in the

chocolate shop, I'll sail to the tropical kingdom first. Put the time I spent in Glenridge behind me.

For one split-second, I imagine Etta at my side, standing on the deck of my ship with a warm, tropical breeze blowing through her hair. She's wearing her breeches with that billowy shirt she favors tucked tight at her waist, and I have my arm wrapped around her back.

I blink the thought away and force myself to focus on the present. But presently, I would rather be at sea than in this carriage.

The ride back to Rynvale has taken hours, and Kerrick's had his eyes on Etta almost the entire time. Every once in a while, to break up the monotony, he shifts a scowl at me.

I'm getting the distinct impression that His Highness doesn't like me very much.

But Sabine...well, the princess likes me enough. When she's not trying to fill the carriage with lighthearted small talk or sending pitying smiles at Etta, she's watching me from the corner of her eye, curious.

I have no room in my head for Sabine past a fleeting thought. I'm too consumed with whether Etta is warm enough with her wet hair. Or if Etta has glanced at me again. Or, perhaps, if Etta meant to place her hand between us, right there, so close to my leg.

What a ridiculous fool this infatuation makes a man. I feel like a bumbling schoolboy about to kiss a girl for the first time, but unable to figure out what to do with my wretched hands.

The carriage finally stops in the courtyard in front of the castle, and the king's men scurry out to greet us. They remain expressionless as they help Etta down the steps, but I have no doubt there will be gossip in the servant's quarters later. It's not every day a beautiful young woman shows up looking more like a drowned rat than the mysterious marquise she's rumored to be.

When we enter the castle, eyes linger on Etta, and people lean close, murmuring speculations between them. One quick glance at the girl tells me she's overwhelmed.

"I'm afraid my lady is quite exhausted from this dreadful ordeal," I say to the king.

His Majesty nods. "Of course."

He snaps his fingers, and, immediately, a steward runs forward. They exchange quick words, and then a maid materializes from a hall door and sweeps Etta away. I start to follow, but Kerrick shoots me a look so full of warning, I decide it's in everyone's best interest if I stay put.

The last thing I want is to start a duel right here with the crown prince in the middle of the hall. It would be a shame to best him in front of his people...and a good way to get myself booted out of the castle altogether.

In fact, the best thing to do is show Etta as little attention as possible. She laughs at something the maid has told her, and she disappears around the corner.

I clear my throat and pull my eyes away.

CHAPTER 29

A MAID CINCHES ME UP SO TIGHTLY, I SWEAR I WON'T BE ABLE to draw in a breath. After I'm trussed more securely than a roasting hen, another maid lowers an elaborate gown over my head. With my hands up in the air, I feel like a child, but I don't make a fuss. The pair seems to know what they're doing, and I certainly don't...and they don't need to know that.

After what must be another half hour of fussing, I barely recognize myself in the mirror. They've brushed my hair to a shine and elaborately piled it on top of my head. My gown is pale lavender and gold, so beautiful I'm scared to touch it. My skin is pink from the tortuous scrubbing I endured. The whole time they murmured that it must have been some mud puddle I stumbled into to have become so filthy. As they worked, I shivered in that scalding hot water, terrified they'd notice that my skin isn't as soft as it should be, that it's too dark from my hours in the sun. Polite or oblivious, they said nothing.

"Is there anything else we can do for you, my lady?"

I shake my head, dismissing them. It's only when they

shut the door behind them that I realize I'm alone, virtually a prisoner in this very lovely room. My eyes sweep over the quarters that are to be mine for several days, longer if the king has his way.

I've never seen so much fabric in my life. The draperies, bed covers, canopy, and rugs are all done in the palest of blues. There are pillows—huge, fluffy pillows—adorning the bed, and even though I never nap during the day, I can't think of anything more lovely than crawling upon them and sleeping until the next morning. Since I don't know how I'd manage it in this gown, I refrain. With nothing to stop Puss, he's asleep in the very center of the bed. He stretches, content, and rolls to his other side.

Upholstered benches and soft-looking chairs dot the room, along with a table that's just large enough for taking tea. A fireplace sits asleep on the side wall, and a bookcase stands next to it.

Everything is sleek, scrolling dark wood with accents of silver.

It takes several moments to take it all in, and I stand here, gaping at the finery around me. I can imagine the looks on Eugene and Thomas's faces if they could see me now.

Oh, no.

I have to send word to Eugene. He'll worry when I don't return by late this evening and have rounded up a search party by morning.

With purpose, I push my door open and peer into the hall. I shut it softly, imagining that's what a marquise would do, and then set off to find Beau. I wander for the longest time, enjoying the way my heels click on the marble floor and studying the art. I'm hopelessly lost, but there are far worse pastimes than wandering the palace in a beautiful gown.

Finally, a helpful manservant with kind eyes takes pity on me and asks, "Are you turned about, my lady?"

"Dreadfully so."

He smiles and ushers me down this hallway and then another. We wind down a staircase, take another hall, and suddenly I've arrived in the royal family's sitting room.

"Suzette!" His Majesty exclaims as he stands and takes my hands. "How much better you look."

I bob my head in greeting, not sure what to do since he has my hands. "Thank you for your kindness."

Releasing me, he waves my words away. "Think nothing of it. It's all to my pleasure, I must admit, because I have been waiting so very eagerly to meet you."

Kerrick stands behind him, and a muscle in his jaw twitches. He wears a smile, but he's as nervous as I am that I'll be found out.

Beau sits in the corner on a settee, speaking with Sabine, seemingly unconcerned. I wait for him to look over, to send me some unspoken message of encouragement, but he seems to be too busy with the princess.

A twinge of unease pierces me, but I brush it away and smile at the king.

"Now that I see you, mademoiselle," the king says, "I must say—I'm struck with the strangest feeling of déjà vu."

My answering laugh is high-pitched, just a touch hysterical. Kerrick's face goes white, which doesn't help a bit.

"I have one of those faces," I finally answer. "I hear it often."

His Majesty narrows his eyes and strokes his chin. Slowly, he shakes his head as he frowns. "No, I don't think so."

"Father," Kerrick finally jumps in. "I'm sure we'd both remember if we'd been introduced to someone as lovely as the marquise."

"Ah, that is a good point." The king finally nods, smiling.

"If you'll forgive me for saying so, my lady, you're quite enchanting. How is it you've hidden yourself away all these years?"

"I...well..."

Hearing my floundering, Beau finally looks over. He goes still, his mouth parting just slightly. I forget the king's question as our eyes meet, and I flush, suddenly self-conscious of the modern cut of the gown, the way it dips lower than I'm used to and tugs in so very tightly at my waist.

The way Beau's looking at me almost...well, it almost seems as if...

"What does it matter?" Kerrick asks his father, his back to Beau so he thankfully doesn't witness the exchange. "She's here now." The prince's smile is a little indulgent, but he's mostly irritated with his father's line of questioning. Before the king can say anything else, Kerrick extends his arm. "May I take you on a tour, Suzette? Show you the gardens, perhaps?"

I jump at the chance to be away from the king's curious gaze. Still slightly unnerved, I avoid Beau as Kerrick leads me away.

With a nod of the prince's head, the people loitering in the garden make themselves scarce. As soon as we're alone, Kerrick turns to me and lets out a deep breath. Though he appears relieved for the moment, his shoulders remain tense.

"I watched the whole thing unfold before my eyes," he says, rubbing his hands up and down my exposed lower arms as if he thinks I'm cold, "and I still don't quite understand how it is that you're here."

"I don't either." I let my gaze wander to a bed of deep red roses at the edge of the garden. "And I'm afraid I'm going to be found out at any moment."

Kerrick murmurs his agreement, but he seems distracted. His hands go still on my arms when the sound of a gardener nearby reaches our ears. Too easily spooked, we stay like this, frozen, but the footsteps fade away. After several minutes, the prince gently tilts my chin toward him, reclaiming my attention. "I am glad you're here."

It feels as if it's been so long since Kerrick's touched me, though in truth it was only a month ago that we parted. Not that long, really, but his hands feel foreign. Smiling, I step back and pretend to study a tall rosemary plant to my left.

How many girls has the prince escorted through these very garden paths? How many princesses, just like Sabine, has he had on his arm in this short time since we said our goodbyes?

On that train of thought, I say, "Sabine has been here for quite some time." I watch a large, fat bee rise from one flower, circle the buttercup next to it several times, and then sink into the yellow center. "I thought you said she was only one in a parade of girls."

Kerrick clears his throat, uncomfortable. "My father is fond of her."

I nod.

"But I think he's fonder of you." Kerrick sets his hand on my shoulder. "In fact, perhaps I should be concerned that he'll want to keep you for himself."

Unable to help myself, I laugh. Kerrick knows very well that the king, though extremely attentive, has certainly not shown any of that kind of interest.

"Since we're on the subject of people who are fond of you," the prince continues, "why is Beau here?"

The way Kerrick phrases the question takes me by surprise. And I don't have an answer for him. Ever since Beau came to Rynvale the first time with Puss, he's dedicated himself to the plan. How does he benefit? His chocolate shop has been closed more than it's been open.

Is he that eager to see me marry Kerrick? Does he think, perhaps, that I'll compensate him once I'm queen?

"He's only a friend," I say. "And I wouldn't be here if it weren't for his help."

Kerrick's brow wrinkles, but he doesn't argue or ask me to send the chocolatier away.

"There you are!" Sabine calls from the entrance.

With Beau on her arm, the princess sweeps into the garden. Her gown is the most ridiculous thing I've ever seen. The pink fabric shimmers in the sunlight, and the skirt is so full, I have no idea how she fits through a doorway. Her little dog trails behind her, obviously terrified of wandering too far from her voluminous skirts.

Kerrick steps forward to greet her, obviously relieved that she's arrived to end the tense conversation. She frees Beau and clasps the prince's hands before she gives him a chastising look. "You mustn't overtire Suzette. I'm sure she's exhausted."

Not looking back at me, Kerrick nods.

While the two are preoccupied, I step near Beau and whisper, "Eugene will panic when I don't return tonight."

"I've already ridden to Glenridge and back while you were 'resting.'"

Surprised, I ask, "How did—"

I stop abruptly when I notice that Kerrick's staring at the two of us, his eyes slightly narrowed.

"How are you feeling?" Sabine turns her attention to me and wrinkles her brow, overly concerned. "No one will think any less of you if you decide to retire to your room for the evening."

I glance at Kerrick, who's still wearing that odd expression. Slowly, I nod. "I am, quite suddenly, very tired. I think it might be for the best."

The princess nods, sympathetic. "Of course. I'll make sure someone brings your dinner to your rooms."

If she wasn't smiling so sweetly, I would swear she was trying to get rid of me for the evening. But she just watches me with her violet eyes, looking as innocent as a fawn.

"I'll walk you," Beau offers, already stepping forward.

Kerrick immediately tenses. "That's all right. I'll take the marquise."

Beau's gaze goes between us, but after several seconds, he steps back and shrugs as if indifferent. "Of course."

The prince takes my arm, but he lingers in the garden for several minutes more, talking to Sabine about the gazebo she requested be fitted with a sunshade. I take the time to subtly turn my attention to Beau. My eyes run over his hair, which is in desperate need of a trim. I study the width of his shoulders and the impatient way he drums his fingers on his leg.

I wait for the slight stir of butterflies that I felt earlier, but my stomach is quite at ease.

Kerrick finishes his conversation. With a relieved sigh, I look away from Beau and allow the prince to escort me to my room.

CHAPTER 30

Etta

I STAND ON MY BALCONY AND LOOK OUT PAST THE CITY. THE moon has just risen. It's almost full tonight, and it illuminates the countryside in silver light. I've never been up this high, never seen the land like this. In the moonlight, the forest is black, the meadows are gray, and the creeks and a nearby lake twinkle like stars.

The world looks so vast from up here. Standing here, looking at this small sliver of the kingdom, makes me realize there's so little I've seen.

"It's not very becoming of a lady to stand on her balcony dressed only in her shift," Puss says from behind me.

Rolling my eyes, I step inside and lock the door behind me. "There was no one about, cat."

"That you know of."

Earlier, as the day faded into night, my panic began to grow. There's no way I won't be found out. I have no way to prove the title that Puss made up. At best, I will be sent back to the mill, forgotten and never heard from again. At worst, I may find myself in the stocks, possibly the dungeons.

Fear rises in my chest, and I take a deep breath.

I rub my throbbing temples and glare at Puss. "They're going to find us out."

"They won't." The cat stretches on the bed.

Taking a step closer, I say, "They will! I don't know how to be a marquise. I'm going to make a misstep somewhere, and it's going to end badly for all of us. The king is already questioning me."

Unconcerned, Puss yawns and then closes his eyes, informing me that this conversation is over.

I pace back and forth, nervous. I can't share my concerns with Kerrick; he's already too uneasy. I can't speak with Beau because Kerrick never leaves us alone. I don't even know where the chocolatier's staying. They could have put him in the servant's quarters for all I know. Though surely they wouldn't. He has more right to be here than I do.

At least, I think he does. I still know very little about him.

A quiet knock sounds at my balcony door, and I jump. My pulse skips and then begins to race. We're several stories in the air, and there are no stairs that lead to the ground. I must be hearing things. I begin to relax marginally until there's another knock.

I glance at Puss, unsure what to do. The cat's slept through the noise. My crossbow's still somewhere near the creek where I left it. Even if I had it, I'm not sure I could actually shoot someone. And what if it's not a "someone" at all? Perhaps it's only a hobgoblin, bored in the kitchens and amusing itself by playing tricks on me. But what if it's something more sinister...

Should I run into the hall, find a guard? Ignore the knock and hope whatever it is goes away?

"Etta!" a voice on the other side calls.

Immediately, feeling ridiculous, I pull on a dressing robe, unlock the doors, and swing them open. Beau stands on the balcony, arms crossed. A slow smile builds on his face, the teasing type that's just crooked enough to be endearing. And, so help me, my heart stutters, just like it did earlier.

I stand here, gaping at him.

"Do you think you might invite me in?" he asks, his voice rich with suppressed laughter. "Or should I stand here at the threshold?"

"Oh!" I say when I realize I'm blocking the doorway, staring at him. I step aside. "Of course." Before I close the door, I, again, peer out at the balcony. "How did you get out there?"

Beau leans a hip against the settee and points a thumb toward the door. "I climbed the lattice from the terrace below."

"But *why?*"

He frowns, not paying me much attention, and studies a book on the end table. "I couldn't convince anyone to tell me where they'd placed you. When I saw you on the balcony, I figured this was the easiest way to see you."

I glance out the window. The terrace is three stories down. The lattice is most assuredly not the easiest way. I give him a pointed look.

Beau answers my silent question with a shrug. He opens the book's cover and thumbs through the first few pages. "That, and I didn't think you wanted your prince to know I made a midnight visit."

The words, though spoken lightly, hang between us, thickening the air.

When I don't answer, Beau flips the book closed and looks at me. "What is it? You look like you've swallowed a toad."

I let out a long sigh. "It's just been a long day. My mind is all jumbled."

"You need sleep," he says.

Feeling listless, I nod.

"Are you all right?" He frowns. It takes him three steps to close the distance between us. Once he reaches me, he presses his palm to my forehead. "That creek water must have been frigid."

I go still under Beau's hand, and my gaze meets his. My breath catches, and I sense the moment he notices. His eyes widen marginally, and his fingers jump against my skin. Then, as if I've burned him, he takes an abrupt step backward and clears his throat.

An awkward silence stretches between us.

"Take me home, Beau," I say after several moments. Turning from him, I study an upholstered chair. The pale silk is cool to the touch, and I trace my finger over the silver threads that have been woven into the fabric. "I don't belong here."

Beau shakes his head, looking muddled. "Take you home? We just got here."

"I'm living a lie, and I hate it. I'd rather spend all my life in the loft of Eugene's cottage than pretend I'm someone I'm not."

He seems to think my words over, and indecision shadows his expression. After several long heartbeats, he says, "You'll feel better in the morning. Sleep on it, Etta."

"You think I should stay?" I ask, somewhat startled.

With Kerrick.

It's unspoken, but the words linger between us.

Slowly, expressionless, Beau nods. "Of course I think you should stay."

"They're going to find out!" I whirl around. "How couldn't they? The Carabas name means *nothing*."

He looks at the carpet and then glances back at me from the corner of his eye. "That's not exactly true."

"What do you mean?"

"You should sit," he says as he directs me to the bench.

After drawing in a deep breath, Beau explains.

"Are you telling me"—I poke a finger at his chest—"that you shared all this with the *cat* but not with me?"

Helpless, he attempts to smile. "I'm telling you now."

I run a hand through my loose hair and clench my eyes shut. "That explains why you're helping me. Because you need Puss to take you to your family's estate." I open my eyes. "I'm using your family name! Why are you allowing that?"

He leans forward, his expression earnest. "I've thought this through, and it works well, actually. I plan on going back to the sea as soon as I've cleared up this unfortunate ogre situation, and you need somewhere to live. Pose as the marquise. *Be* the marquise. You'll have everything you could ever need or want, and you can choose whomever you want to marry instead of picking the most convenient person."

Blinking a little too fast, I sink farther into the bench. "You *are* leaving."

"I, well…yes, that's my plan." For a moment I think he's going to reach out, but then he crosses his arms tightly against his chest.

Slowly, my surprise morphs into irritation. "And you'll just give me your family's name and estate?"

"Not give, exactly. More like leave you as a caretaker."

Overwhelmed, I stand and toss my hands in the air. "Why even bother with the ogre if your land means so little to you? Why didn't you just stay at sea?"

Beau winces at my tone, which is not altogether cordial. "It's my family home, Etta. I cannot allow it to be overrun with vile beasts." He stands and sets a tentative hand on my arm. "This was important to my father. He didn't have a chance to tend to it before he passed. But I intend to."

I wait several moments, studying Beau, before I say, "I would have helped you without the deception."

"It was more of an omission." A smile plays at his lips. "And here I thought *I* was helping *you*."

And just like that, my anger slips away. "Fine. We'll stay here tomorrow, just as we said we would. And when we leave, we will force Puss to take us to your land."

"Thank you, Etta," he says, his voice quiet in the still room.

I shrug one shoulder and turn away from him, unable to meet his eyes. "Of course."

CHAPTER 31

Sabine and I have embroidered for hours—literally, from the time we finished breakfast, stopping only briefly for tea, and then we resumed after lunch. The princess doesn't seem to notice the day passing us by, but I take frequent glances out the window, wishing I were outside. This is as tortuous as mending all day.

"Your stitches are very precise," Sabine says as she peeks at my work.

By 'precise,' she probably means 'simplistic.' Though my mother taught me needlework when I was little, it's not an art I've had much time to practice in the last few years. I use the most basic stitches, making a few meandering leaves and stems over my handkerchief. I've already knotted my thread more times than I can count, and every time I have to flip the piece over and untangle it, Sabine's brow creases ever so slightly, and she looks confused as to why I'm having so much trouble with it.

Another fifteen minutes. Another glance out the window.

This time, there's something more interesting to look at than the gardens.

"What are they doing?" I ask Sabine as I stand to get a better look at Kerrick and Beau.

Sabine finally sets her embroidery aside to join me and smiles radiantly. "They're going to play court tennis."

I want to ask her what that is, but since Beau obviously knows, I don't dare ask.

"Let's go watch them," she says.

Glad to leave my handkerchief behind, I follow Sabine through the castle and to the gardens. When the servants see us coming, chairs and a sunshade immediately materialize. Autumn flowers sit on the tiny table between us, a lovely assortment of orange and purple chrysanthemums.

"Tea, mademoiselles?" a maid asks. "Something cool, perhaps?"

Sabine fluffs out her huge skirts—sunshine yellow today, scoops her little dog onto her lap, and scratches him under his chin. "Tea would be lovely."

I nod in agreement, and the girl rushes off.

A net has been stretched out, and the men stand on opposite sides. A roofed garden wall looms to the left, and both Kerrick and Beau hold a racket. The men smile when they see us, but they're obviously too consumed with thoughts of besting the other to come over.

Sabine, sensing that the game is foreign to me, quietly explains the rules as we watch. They play with a palm-sized cork ball, which they knock back and forth with the rackets. Beau, despite Kerrick's best efforts, seems to be winning.

"I want to try it," I say to Sabine.

She laughs out loud. "It's a man's sport."

I'd rather be here than inside, stitching more leaves, but the game loses some of its appeal when I realize I'm stuck on the sidelines.

The match, which started out as somewhat friendly, progressively becomes more competitive. In the heat of the late afternoon, the men roll up their sleeves. Sweat glistens from their brows and servants bring them water each time they pause.

Rolling a napkin in my lap, I say to Sabine, "They're taking this rather seriously, aren't—"

Before I can finish the words, Beau hits a stray ball back with force. Kerrick, expecting Beau to have missed, doesn't move quickly enough, and the cork ball collides with his face. The prince drops his racket and stumbles back, holding a hand over the injury. Obviously in a great deal of pain, he lowers himself onto a nearby stone bench.

Sabine's up in a flash, running toward the prince. Beau is already leaning over him, apologizing even though, in my opinion, it was more Kerrick's fault for not being prepared.

Beau steps back as the princess pushes her way between them. She kneels in front of Kerrick and tuts over the wound, which is already beginning to swell.

"I'm fine," Kerrick mutters, but he doesn't push her away.

Several servants rush forward to assist the prince. Sabine bats them away, puts her arm around Kerrick's back, and escorts the prince toward the castle's entrance.

Beau offers one more apology and winces slightly as Kerrick grumbles that there's no real harm done. The gaggle of servants follows the prince inside, and once they're gone, the gardens are unusually quiet. Beau and I stare at the rose-covered arch they disappeared through. Then, unable to help myself, I begin to giggle. I clamp my hand over my mouth, embarrassed. A swift smile crosses Beau's face, but he too quickly composes himself.

"Shouldn't you be the one nursing his wounds?" Beau asks after several moments.

I think about his question, but I have no answer.

KERRICK'S EYE IS A NASTY SHADE OF PURPLE AND YELLOW, AND I can hardly look at it. We're dining at the king's table, and I'm doing everything possible to avoid the strange two-pronged fork utensils the others are using. So far I've lingered over soup and bread.

Noticing my hesitance to eat anything substantial, the king leans forward from his spot at the head of the table. "Are you feeling well, Suzette? You haven't caught ill, have you?"

I set my spoon aside and place my hands in my lap. "No, Your Majesty. I'm afraid I'm a little overtired."

He frowns. "I was worried you'd spent too much time in the sun. Perhaps you should stay tomorrow, as well. An extra day of rest could do you good."

Too much time in the sun? I was only outside during the men's tennis match. The rest of the day was filled with Sabine's favorite things: drawing (which I learned I'm horrible at), singing (which I'm adequate, though the sheet music was foreign to me), playing cards (which was entertaining at first but quickly became dull), and embroidery. Of course.

"I appreciate your kind offer," I say. "But I must be going tomorrow."

The king argues and cajoles, but I stand firm. Beau informed His Majesty that he received word that my men "caught" the bandits and rescued my maid, so there is no reason for him to detain me further.

If I stay here another day, I'll go mad.

The thought is sobering. If I were to marry Kerrick, if everything goes as Puss has planned, and I stay, would this be my life?

And what of Beau's offer? Could I stay on his estate after he leaves? Do as I please?

I glance down at my clasped hands. In my lap, I've

scrunched a linen napkin in my fists. Now, I do my best to smooth the wrinkles from it.

The king retires after dinner. As soon as he's away, Beau asks Sabine if she would care to walk in the gardens. I know he's trying to give me a moment with Kerrick, but I feel a twinge of discomfort when I see the two of them, so handsome together, stride through the doors.

"You're leaving tomorrow?" Kerrick asks once we're alone. "Are you sure?"

"I think it's best if we cut this visit short," I say.

The prince nods, his mouth turned into a slight frown as if he's sad to see me go. But his eyes are relieved.

"When will you return?" he asks. Then, sensing my hesitation, Kerrick leans forward. "You will return, won't you, Etta?"

Again, I twist the napkin in my lap. I focus on it, avoiding Kerrick's eyes. "I'm not sure this was wise."

I stare at the wrinkled fabric, waiting for him to say something. He shifts in his seat, takes a sip from his chalice, rubs a hand over his face.

Finally, he says, "You're right."

A sliver of disappointment stabs my heart. I expected some argument from him at least.

Kerrick sets his hand over mine, making me go still. Sensing he's waiting for me to meet his gaze, I slowly raise my eyes to his.

"Etta…" He looks more serious than I've ever seen him, so solemn. So kingly. "I care for you."

But.

"It's all right," I whisper. "You don't have to do this. We've already said our goodbyes."

Kerrick grimaces and closes his eyes.

I stand. "I'm sorry."

The prince lets me go, sits as still as a statue as I lay my hand briefly on his shoulder. The only sound is the echo of my heels clicking against the marble floor as I leave.

Before I slip through the doors, I take one last glance at Kerrick. His elbow rests on the table, and he leans his forehead against his fist. A short lock of golden hair falls across his temple, framing his face. Instead of anguished, he looks a little sad, a little confused.

Apparently, goodbyes become easier the more times you do them because I feel the same way.

I'm halfway down the hall when Kerrick calls for me. I turn back, startled. He jogs past the decorative suits of armor, past the art and dozens of vases filled with flowers.

"What will you do now? Will you go back to Eugene's mill?" he asks when he reaches me.

"I…" I shrug. "Eventually…perhaps. But, for now, I'm going to travel with Beau to his family's land."

Kerrick's eye—the one that isn't blackened— twitches. "Oh."

"It's not like that," I say in a rush, though as I hear the words, I wonder. Do I want it to be? Pushing the thought aside, I continue, "He needs my help."

Actually, Beau needs my cat's help. Not mine.

Kerrick crosses his arms, and his face is once again thoughtful. "With what?"

It's not my secret to tell.

I shake my head and set my hand on his. "It's a family matter."

"And, yet, he's included you." The prince raises his brows.

Sighing, I stand on my toes and press my lips to his cheek. "Goodbye, Kerrick."

This time, he lets me go.

CHAPTER 32

Etta

"So what exactly does an ogre look like?" I ask as we near the land that Puss declares belongs to Beau.

The cat isn't pleased with us, but the small beast apparently has a noble streak because he's honoring his promise.

"To you?" Puss asks from my lap. He stretches, trying to make himself more comfortable from his precarious position atop the new, extremely lovely, palomino mare Beau bought me for our travels. "He's enchanted himself as a man. But I can't tell you what manner of man, or what age."

Beau rides next to me, and a myriad of emotions cross his face. One moment he's eager, the next anxious, and every once in a while, he looks as if he'd rather abandon the whole mission and turn toward the west, riding until he meets the sea.

"What does he look like to you?" I ask.

The cat's whiskers twitch. "Grotesque, sallow skin bulging at his joints, beady eyes too small for his head, a cap of sparse bristly hair that looks as if he robbed it from a pig."

"So you've seen him before?" I ask, curious now that we're

closer. The description makes me nervous, makes my stomach tie itself in knots.

"I have."

We've ridden most of the day, and I'm growing saddle-weary. I shift, causing Puss to readjust himself again, which in turn causes him to look put out. I'm about to suggest the cat make use of his own four paws but we reach the top of the hill, and the words fade before they pass my lips. In the distance, a castle sits on the next rise. It's large, numerous windows are made gold by the evening sun.

It's an impressive structure, not as large as King Deloge's, but massive all the same. Even from this distance, I can make out the black and yellow flags atop the turrets. They flutter in the breeze, lazy and unconcerned. Twinkling afternoon sunlight reflects off a moat that winds around the structure. The drawbridge is down, and a donkey-pulled cart slowly makes its way under the portcullis.

Puss rises and pads forward on the saddle. "There it is."

I take in the rich fields, the vineyards, the dense expanse of forest that stretches to the rear of the estate. "Surely this is not Carabas land."

No ogre lives here. Where are the thorned vines, covering the walls? Where are the dark and sinister gargoyles, the blackened trees, and the pale, gray-hued skies?

This land is fertile, kissed by the sun.

The cat nods to a farmer and his wife who toil not-so-far-away in a wheat field that's overdo for harvesting. At first glance, I see nothing out of the ordinary. But when they look up, curious to see who passes, I notice their gaunt faces, their tired eyes. Everyone has the same look, the same hopeless, broken expression.

"What has happened to them, Puss?"

"Their master in an ogre," the cat answers. "I think the question is rather self-explanatory."

I suppose it is.

We reach the gates just as the sun sinks behind the trees to the west. The sky is still aglow, but there's the promise of night in the air. Wood-smoke rises from the chimneys of thatched cottages, and a delicious aroma wafts from inside the castle's gates.

My stomach growls, now used to eating regular meals, protesting our lack of lunch. As if having the same thought, Puss jumps to the ground and disappears into the brush. It's an inconvenient time for him to go mousing.

Beau's mouth is pressed in a firm line, but his eyes are wide with surprise. Obviously, his father's land is greater than he had anticipated. He pulls his horse to a halt just in front of the drawbridge.

A guard steps forward. He wears a black and yellow tabard over his white, billowing shirt, the crest on his chest matching the one that hangs over the front gates. With a twinge of regret, I admire his functional cavalier hat, black and simple. I had grown rather fond of mine, and now it's gone, left behind at the creek.

My neck is hot, red from being exposed to the sun all day. The ridiculous hat that I wear now, though it matches my gown exquisitely with its peacock plumage and swaths of silk, sits at an angle, shadowing my face but exposing my neck. My hair, curled with irons heated in the fire by a maid from His Majesty's castle this morning, is set in tight ringlets, drawn up and clasped at the side of the nape of my neck, offering no protection whatsoever.

"State your business," the guard says. He eyes Beau, and then his eyes wander over me. I sit a little straighter, hoping to look prim.

"I have come to call on the Marquis of Carabas," Beau says, just as Puss had instructed. "I am a distant relation of his, and we have traveled many weeks."

I wait for the slightest sign of recognition. I'm disappointed, however. The guard only furrows his brow, looking perplexed. "I am afraid, monsieur, you have found the wrong estate. Monsieur Mattis is the lord of these lands."

Beau looks taken aback, and I have to say, he plays it very well. "Are you quite sure?"

The guard's thick, dark eyebrows draw together further. "Yes, Monsieur. No one by the name of Carabas lives here."

Beau and I exchange mock worried glances, and I let my shoulders droop. "Where will we stay the night? The sun has already set."

I'm to play Beau's younger sister, his charge to care for since the unfortunate and untimely deaths of our beloved parents. This part of Puss's plan hits a little too close to home.

"Perhaps," Beau says, leaning forward, "we could beg upon the goodwill of your master? We'll stay a night and be on our way."

The guard frowns, looking muddled. Like he's forgotten something important, and it's just out of reach. I pause, suddenly realizing that perhaps there's something I've forgotten as well.

Why are we here if this is not Beau's family's estate? The man said it belonged to Monsieur Mattis...but Puss said... well, now I don't quite remember what Puss said.

A cool breeze blows from the mountains, a cold, almost arctic wind that promises winter is only a few months away. The guard, noticing me involuntarily shiver, seems to make up his mind.

"Follow me." He turns on his heel, and we ride across the drawbridge after him. When we leave the soft wood, the horses' hoofbeats sound on the impressive cobblestone courtyard. Great swirls and designs have been worked into the stones with a dark granite that glints with mica. Roses climb the interior of the walls, and, despite the cooling nights, the flowers are lush and full, all blooming in dark crimson.

A short man, standing no taller than my shoulders, steps forward and claims my reins. His hair is brown, but his beard is tinged with white.

I try not to gape at him. At the same time, I try not to avert my gaze to the point that it's noticeable.

But I've only seen the mountain dwarves in Rynvale, and only a few at that. They tend to stay near their quarries.

One quick glance shows me that he is not alone. There are many, possibly more dwarves than men. My eyes wander the courtyard, taking everything in. A young human boy and a girl chase each other near the wall, squealing and laughing with delight. A woman fills her basket with apples from a tree so heavy with the fruits, the branches almost dip to the ground. Not too far away, an entire pig is slowly roasting on a spit over a huge fire.

Again, my stomach cramps with hunger.

People loiter about, most attending their chores but some standing in groups, chatting. Beau's estate was to hold something evil, though I can't quite place what it was at the moment. Surely this is not that place.

Something buzzes next to my ear. Startled, I turn, expecting a bee out past daylight hours, but, instead, a whir of green dives into a tall tree next to me. I peer into the branches, and there, on a limb, sits a tiny, winged child. I gape at her, and, shyly, she flits to a closer branch, hiding behind it, peering at me with wide, curious eyes. She does this several times, moving closer with each illuminated step, until she's close enough I could reach out and touch her if I so wished.

My attention is so consumed with the child fairy; I almost miss the entrance of our host.

He's an unassuming man, taller than me but not by much. His once-brown hair is peppered with gray, and his face is round and merry. Though he's not tall in stature, there is no doubt he is the master of this estate. His doublet is rich velvet, and his hunting boots are fine. He wears a rapier, but, like Kerrick, it looks like an accessory more than a necessity.

Immediately, the man smiles at us, but there's something about him...something I should remember. Still, I find myself returning his smile, grasping his offered hand, and swinging from my horse.

"My lady." He bows low. "It is an honor. I am Ettiene Mattis, and you are very welcome here."

Beau hands his horse to another dwarven stableman, but his eyes are on Lord Mattis. He looks conflicted, his expression a mirror to my own internal thoughts. He quickly hides the expression when the man turns to him, and they exchange their own greetings.

"Monsieur Mattis, I am Beauregard Marchand," Beau says, leaving off the Carabas title, exactly as Puss instructed. "And I'm afraid we are rather lost. You see, I am a distant relative of the Carabas family, and we thought this was their land. Have you heard of them? Are we close?"

"Please, call me Ettiene," the lord replies. "And as for the estate you are looking for, you have found it. I'm afraid the Carabas line dwindled long ago, and the land passed to me through my mother, a daughter of the last marquis."

No, that's not right, but Beau is nodding, obviously as confused as I am.

"So you see," Ettiene continues, breaking into a wide smile. "We are cousins, and I insist you and your wife stay."

Beau glances at me, his expression unreadable. "My sister and I would be very grateful."

It's the plan, just as Puss instructed, but I don't like

playing Beau's sister. From the look on his face, it seems he might not care for it either. But it's the cat's plan, not ours.

But why did we need a plan? I don't remember...

And where did Puss go? I glance around the courtyard, looking for the tawny beast, but he seems to have made himself scarce.

To myself, I shake my head, trying to clear the muddled feeling.

Beau motions me forward, and I follow Ettiene through the heavy double-doors. The wood is inlaid with thick iron scrollwork, beautiful and functional, should there be an attack.

We step into an entry foyer so large and grand, I suck in a breath. A huge chandelier hangs from the ceiling, already lit with dozens of tapered candles. Two sets of stairs lead up, one on each side of the room, and they join in a landing on the second floor.

It's cleaner than I expected for an ogre's castle.

The thought is so jarring, I stop abruptly on the stairs and Beau knocks into me from behind. Like a fog evaporating in the heat of day, my brain clears.

Ettiene is the ogre. That's why we're here.

I've fallen prey to the monster's magic, didn't realize I was at risk. Even now, wisps of deception lick at my mind, trying to deceive me again. I blink, attempting to keep my mind clear.

From the top of the stairs, Ettiene pauses and turns back. "Are you all right, Suzette?"

My eyes fly to his. He wears a warm, paternal smile, and for a moment, the magic almost claims me again. It's a clever disguise. As I nod and hurry after him, I study the man. If I concentrate enough, will I be able to see his true form?

Apparently, whatever he conceals himself with is stronger than the curse over the estate, because there isn't even the slightest flicker in his appearance. And for that, I'm grateful. I'm not sure I want to see the monster hiding underneath.

He leads us to an intimate dining hall. I hesitate before trying the food before me, wondering if it's enchanted as well. It looks like chicken, but what if it's rat? Algae? What exactly does an ogre's diet consist of?

Ettiene watches, and I take a tentative bite, using a pronged fork similar to the one I avoided while staying with Kerrick. I chew carefully, concentrating on the texture in particular. After several moments, I am quite sure it is, in fact, chicken. Relieved, and still starving, I take another bite.

Satisfied, Ettiene begins to tell us about the estate. Beau listens, his eyebrows knitting every now and then when his mind tries to free itself from the ogre's magic. So far, I don't believe he's been successful. The ogre asks many questions about the sea, and Beau is happy to oblige him with answers.

Instead of listening, I take in the room. A large chandelier hangs central over the table, and more candles flicker from its scrolling iron branches. The draperies are velvet, black, and drawn, shutting out the evening air. There's a stillness in the room, the feeling of being closed-in. Like, perhaps, the windows are never opened to the fresh air.

Two human guards stand at the entrance of the room, waiting to attend their master should their services be required. We're served by dwarven women—stout, handsome females. They wear their hair plaited under caps; some have twisted the braids into tidy buns, but more wear the tails long, falling down their backs and landing near their waists.

"It was very good," I say to one as she comes to take my plate.

"I'll tell the cook, mademoiselle." Her eyes dart to my face, but she quickly looks back to her hands, where she efficiently wipes a stray crumb from my setting and places a bowl of hot water with a slice of some sort of citrus in front of me.

At a loss, I look to Beau for guidance. Subtly, he meets my eyes and dips his hands in the water. After he's swished them around a bit, he takes the tiny towel and dries them. The dwarf at his side whisks the bowl away and then places yet another bowl. This one, I'm sure, is filled with soup.

I follow Beau's lead through the meal, watching him the entire time, waiting for him to overcome the magic. There are several times I think he's quite close.

Finally, dinner comes to an end. Ettiene excuses himself, leaving yet another dwarf to lead us to our rooms. Before we leave the dining hall, I look again for Puss, wondering what has become of him.

"This way," our dwarven guide says.

She walks with purpose, striding out of the dining hall at a brisk pace. We follow, lingering as far back as possible.

Beau matches his pace with mine, close enough our shoulders rub. "I have a horrible headache. I feel as if my brain is in a fog."

"Ogre magic," I answer at a bare whisper, glancing around to see if there are any ears nearby.

Now that I know there are fairies and dwarves, it's hard to tell what lurks in these halls.

The moment I say the words, Beau's mouth drops open, and he clenches his eyes shut. When he opens them again, the horror that he was deceived by the magic is plain to see on his face.

"I was taken in by it as well," I assure him.

We follow the woman the rest of the way in silence. As we go, I take in the castle. The interior isn't nearly as welcoming as the courtyard. Though the halls are lit by sporadic cande-labras atop tables, the darkness prevails. Art hangs on the walls, but it's too dim to admire the paintings or tapestries.

Everything, however, every nook and cranny, is spotless. Before we arrived, I had imagined dust and cobwebs, spiders and rats. There is none of that here.

"Here you are, monsieur," the woman says, finally stopping in front of a simple door in what seems to be an endless, dark hallway. She inserts a key in the lock, swings the door open, and then hands the key to Beau. Without another word, she nods for me to follow her farther down the hall.

I glance over my shoulder, looking at Beau. His mouth is set in a firm line, but he nods.

We walk farther than I expect. I had hoped my room would be close to Beau's, in the same hall if not next door. It seems that is not to be. We take several more turns. Just when I think we may have made one large circle and are about to find ourselves in the entry, the dwarf stops. Just like before, she unlocks the door, hands me the key, bows her head, and then leaves.

Nervous, I watch as the light the woman carries grows dimmer then disappears altogether as she turns a corner. Once she's out of sight, I push my way into the room. Thankfully, another candelabra sits on a table near the bed, flickering, if not cheerfully, efficiently at least. This chamber is nothing like the light and airy blue room I occupied in the king's castle. Here the furniture is heavy, solid, and the bedposts tower to the ceiling. Atop each post, a wooden gargoyle perches. No matter which way I step, it seems as if their eyes are focused on me. The canopy is made of a thick damask, ornate and dark burgundy, and the bedding has been made to match.

There is a fireplace, but no fire, and a window, but like every other, the drapes are closed. Immediately, I cross the room and pull them back. I am high, several stories in the air, and there is no balcony. How will Puss reach me? Will I be here, alone, all night?

This dim, still room terrifies me.

Just as my throat begins to close with panic, my eyes land on a table near the bed where a second candelabra sits. There's something there. Curiosity quelling my fear, I go toward it. A tiny confection, some kind of fruit tart, sits next to a note and a pair of thick stockings.

"Thank you for your kind words," it reads. *"The castle grows cold at night. I thought you might have a use for these."*

"Kind words?" I muse out loud though there is no one to hear me.

And then it comes to me. The cook. I complimented her food. These must be from her.

I stroke the soft, thick stockings and then clutch them to my chest. My heart swells at the simple gesture that I so needed tonight. These gifts, they can only mean one thing. I bite my lip, my excitement and wonder overwhelming my fear.

I have made friends with a kitchen brownie.

CHAPTER 33

Etta

WE FINALLY FIND PUSS IN THE COURTYARD, HIDING IN AN overgrown kitchen garden. The frost has yet to kill the herbs, and the air is thick with basil, rosemary, and lavender.

"Where have you been?" I demand as I scoop him into my arms and nuzzle the soft fur at his neck.

Puss struggles against me for a moment, more for show than anything, and then settles against me and purrs. "The ogre isn't overly fond of cats."

"You should have warned us about his magic," Beau says, sounding disgruntled.

The cat turns his eyes on him. "I told you he's enchanted this land. What more did you need to know?"

Beau crosses his arms. "That we could be affected by it. I thought it was a onetime spell, affecting those present at the time of the curse. Not us, not now."

Puss turns back to me and rubs his head against my hand. "Now you know. Once you become aware of it, it's easier to fight. Whether I told you or not, you would have struggled at first."

From the corner of my eye, I see another childlike fairy flit toward us, taking cover in the foliage of a lilac bush.

"Puss?" I ask, interrupting their conversation before they begin to quarrel. I drop my voice to a whisper. "Why are there fairies in the garden? Dwarves in the house?"

The cat leaps from my arms and jumps on the back of an iron garden bench. "They are prisoners, collected by the ogre."

"Why do they stay? What keeps them here?" Beau asks.

Puss licks his paw and then begins to groom his face. "It seems that they are locked in by an invisible boundary."

My blood chills. "Are we as well?"

Done grooming, the cat puts his paw down. "Try to leave, and we will see."

We find ourselves in the courtyard. It seems a different place than yesterday. Last night, the roses were welcoming; now they appear sinister. Humans and dwarves look tired, their eyes hooded with shadows. Those who cluster together whisper quietly as if they are afraid of being overheard. There is no laughter, no playing. The children are nowhere to be found.

It was an illusion.

Puss stays to the bushes, trying to keep from drawing attention to himself. "Go on, cross the bridge. If you cannot pass, then you're a prisoner with the rest."

I look at Beau, unsure.

He holds up a hand, stopping me. "No. I'll do it."

As he walks toward the castle's exit, I clasp my hands to keep them still and hold my breath. No one stops him as he steps onto the drawbridge. No one and nothing stops him as he strides across.

And then he's on the other side.

I let out my held breath.

Beau, too, looks relieved, and he walks back over the

drawbridge without incident. We make our way to a less inhabited area of the castle grounds, Puss being careful to stay out of sight. Monsieur Mattis is absent this afternoon, and Beau and Puss begin to talk strategy as to how we're going to rid the estate of the ogre.

None of their ideas sound plausible. Bored, I wander the gardens alone and find many splendorous things: more fairies in the trees, winged fawns in the stables, water sprites in the ponds. The dwarves don't pay me any attention, and I stay out of their way.

I watch them, though. Do they miss their mountains, miss mining for their precious jewels?

As I wind my way down the moss-covered stones, I spot a flash of brown cloak ahead of me. A short figure darts from the vegetable patch, dropping several fingerling potatoes as she flees. One moment she's there; the next she's gone.

To my growing list of fantastic creatures, I add kitchen brownies in the garden.

"Are you enjoying yourself?"

I whip around, clutching my hand to my heart, trying not to imagine the monster behind the man. "Monsieur Ettiene."

"I've startled you." The man looks contrite. As if to make up for it, he offers his arm.

The very last thing I want is to stroll the garden on the arm of a thieving, black-hearted ogre, but I don't see how I have a choice.

The magic hiding his identity is strong; it doesn't waver once. I'm glad for that.

A fairy peers at us from a bush, her already large eyes wide. She flies away as soon as Ettiene glances her way.

"Timid things, aren't they?" he says.

"Why...I mean, how is it you've come to have so many fantastic creatures in your care?" I ask.

"They make me happy."

I wait for him to go on, to give me some excuse as to what they're doing here, but he doesn't continue.

We walk in silence, him taking in the gardens with great interest, tutting when he sees an overgrown topiary. For some reason, the quiet sound of discontent chills me. I wonder what creature will suffer for the plant's lack of care.

Ettiene turns to me abruptly. "I'm glad you've come. I hope you and your"—he pauses and gives me a knowing smile—"brother will stay."

My smile freezes on my face. He doesn't clarify how long he hopes we'll stay, and a heavy feeling settles in the base of my stomach.

"I don't believe we have immediate plans to rush off," I say, trying to laugh lightly.

At odds with the creature I know him to be, the man pats my hand gently and smiles with kind eyes. "I'm glad to hear it."

After several more moments, he excuses himself and strides down another garden path, disappearing through a curtain of willows. The light shines just right, illuminating the leaves, and I can see him through the foliage. Thinking he's just out of sight, Ettiene glances both ways and disappears into a side door leading into the castle.

Wondering what he's up to, I hesitate for only one moment before I decide to follow him.

CHAPTER 34

Beau

"Where did Etta go?" I ask, suddenly realizing I can no longer see her.

Bored with our planning, she began to explore the garden, but she never ventured out of sight. I scan the walkways and nooks, wondering how far she would have gone. A cool, prickly sensation slides up the back of my neck.

If we were anywhere else, if this weren't an ogre's stolen home, I wouldn't worry.

But this isn't anywhere else.

Puss sniffs the air.

"Are you a dog now?" I ask, my voice testy with worry.

The cat glares at me. "I'll have you know cats have a much more sophisticated sense of smell than humans."

"Well, Rufus, do you smell her? Is she close?"

"She was," he answers, ignoring my jab. Then he lets out a low hiss, and the hair on his back stands on end. "And I smell *it*."

He doesn't have to clarify further. I know whom the cat is referring to.

Puss takes off first, but I'm right behind. The gardens are

larger than I imagined, the whole estate is, but we rush through them. It still hasn't quite hit me that this is my land, my castle. It's far more than I expected. Eventually I may sit down and ponder it, but for now, I only want to find Etta.

The cat darts under the low-hanging boughs of a weeping willow, and I push my way through. He stops in front of a door, one so well hidden by ivy and moss that I wouldn't have known it was here if I hadn't been looking for it.

"They went in through here?" I demand, already trying to find the handle. I find a latch and tug on it. The door opens easily, without so much as a creak. My fingers twitch against the hilt of my rapier, eager to be done with this mess but anxious that I might have to use my blade when Etta is involved.

The door opens to stairs and I run up them, feeling an urgency I can't explain. As fast as I move, Puss is faster. I'm almost to the top when a blood-curdling shriek echoes from the chambers above and down the stairwell. I race up the last few stairs, taking them two at a time. As I pass Puss, I draw my sword and burst through the door at the landing.

I slam to a halt, and Puss crashes into my legs. No longer disguised, the ogre stands before us in all his grotesque glory. He towers over me, a giant of a being, and his skin is as sallow as Puss promised. His eyes are black, the whites barely visible, and his hair resembles the bristles of an old, worn broom.

He's backed Etta to the wall and pressed a dagger to her throat. She looks at me with wild eyes, and the color has already drained from her usually lovely face.

"You should tell your 'sister' that curiosity isn't a virtue." The ogre pulls the dagger back abruptly.

Etta draws in a shaky gasp, and her hand flies to her throat. I extend my sword and jerk my head, signaling her to come behind me.

The ogre lets out a series of loud guffaws, grabbing his belly as if it pains him. "You *are* a Carabas, boy. There is no doubt."

I swallow, but I don't lower my sword.

"You're the brother, aren't you? The one the marquis promised would avenge him? You're younger than I expected."

Beside me, Etta stands tall. If I expected her to cower at my back, I was wrong.

"What happened?" I ask her, not taking my eyes off the ogre.

"He was acting suspicious," she says. "So I followed him and saw him change into *that*."

The ogre crosses his arms and smirks, showing off two jutted tusk-like incisors that rise from his bottom jaw. "You think it's comfortable wearing that human cloak day in and day out?" Neither Etta or I know what to say, but it doesn't matter because the ogre's eyes drop to Puss, and he snarls, "Thought I smelled a mangy cat."

Puss hisses and puffs his fur until he's an orange and brown ball of cotton fluff. Not terribly intimidating, to tell you the truth.

"I am the nephew," I interrupt before Puss can do something stupid, like lunge on the monster who could eat him in one bite. "And, yes, I have come to avenge my family's name and take back what is rightfully mine."

The ogre's attention returns to me. Despite the vulgarity that is his appearance, there's a disconcerting air of humanness about him. He sizes me up, and that smug look returns to his face. "The nephew? If you're here, then I suppose it's safe to assume that your dear father is dead?"

Lengthening my sword, I nod.

The creature sits against a massive wooden desk, studying me. "What would be more tragic...killing the last remaining heir to the Carabas line? Or imprisoning him here for the rest of his short, sad human life?"

A chill runs through me, but I refuse to show weakness.

Slowly, the monster smiles. "Imprisonment it is." He turns and waves us out the door. "You're free to go." He glances over his shoulder and grins. "Not too far, of course, but you'll figure that out on your own."

Seeing my chance, I lunge forward. The ogre no more than turns and my sword flies from my grasp, clattering harmlessly against the wall and falling to the floor.

"That's a parlor trick, boy," the ogre says, his eyes and voice somber. "I am the most powerful being that has ever set foot in this kingdom. I do not suggest you test me."

My hand is still extended, and I stand frozen, shocked at the magic that stole my rapier from my grasp. Slowly, I lower my arm.

With a flick of his hand, my sword lifts from the ground and levitates over to him. He holds it gingerly in his gnarled grasp. "Belonged to your father?"

I clench my jaw, refusing to answer him.

"They always do. It's good to keep that poetic tradition alive." He pulls his eyes from the blade and meets my gaze. "Just think of what a prize this will be should you ever best me and win it back."

My temper escalates, hot and impulsive. I'm about to rush him, armed with only my fists, when Etta grasps my arm, pulling me back.

"Not now," she whispers firmly.

Still seething, I turn to her, ready to argue.

Etta's eyes are soft, understanding, but there's a firmness there. A promise that this isn't over. And then she turns to the ogre. "I'm keeping my cat with me from now on."

The ogre smiles and holds out his hands in placation. "I've nothing to hide from him."

She scoops up Puss, who still resembles a livid dandelion, turns abruptly, and marches down the stairs that lead back to the garden. I follow, but before I leave, I glance over my shoulder at the monster I will defeat in the near future.

He looks back, meeting my challenge, and I close the door behind me.

CHAPTER 35

I FIND BEAU IN A HALL, HOLDING A CANDELABRA, STARING AT A portrait of a young man I assume must be his father. The light is dim, as always. All the draperies are shut and the endless candles burn, dripping wax but never snuffing out.

Beau's jaw is tight, and his eyes are hard. He's been inconsolable these last few days—angry and bitter. Now he looks broken.

Silent, I come to stand next to him. His father was handsome, and the artist captured the wanderlust in his eyes. It doesn't surprise me he ventured out to make his own fortune.

Beau must take after his mother, though. The man before him had sandy hair, and his features were mischievous, cunning but without apparent malice. There are enough similarities to make the connection between Beau and his father without ever having met the man, but it's not a resemblance that is uncanny.

"I don't remember what my parents look like," I admit. My voice echoes in the hall, and I wince.

Slowly, blinking as if he just realizes I'm standing with him, Beau turns. "Not at all?"

"It's faded from my memory. Sometimes, a little glimpse of them comes back, but like smoke, it's gone just as quickly." My throat goes thick, and my eyes begin to sting. "Do you think I'll forget Eugene and Thomas?"

As soon as I say the words, a tear spills down my cheek. I grit my teeth and clench my eyes shut, refusing to give in to this.

Beau sets the candelabra on a fern table, places his hands on my arms firmly, and angles me toward him. There's fire in his eyes, a steadfast determination. "I will break this curse."

I want to believe him, but it's been two days since the ogre imprisoned us, and we're no closer than we were the moment we rode over the drawbridge.

"What do you think they'll believe has become of me?" I ask.

"I'll take care of it."

Unable to help myself, I nod and step into his arms. Beau doesn't hesitate this time, unlike so many times before when I've touched him or brushed next to him. He simply wraps his arms around my back and holds me with a fierce protectiveness as I bury my head against his chest.

CHAPTER 36

TIRED OF THE DARK, MUTED CANDLELIGHT, I YANK THE draperies open. Diffused sunlight, white and perfect, shines through the tall, stately window. Outside, snow falls on the distant farms and forests. It's the first snow of the season. I rest my elbows on the sill and set my chin on my palm, my nose itching from the dust I kicked up when I opened the drapes.

We've been at the Carabas estate for nearly two months. The olive greens and yellows of early autumn changed to vibrant reds and oranges, and then the leaves fell. The last that remain, stubborn, immobile, cling to the tree limbs, brown and weathered. Soon they'll be covered with white.

I haven't seen my brothers; I haven't been able to send them word of my whereabouts. Kerrick has no idea where we are either. I would like to think the prince would rescue us if he did, but I'm not sure with how we left things.

A soft noise startles me from my melancholy thoughts, the padding of small feet on the carpet-covered stone floor. I go still, knowing if I turn the visitor will flee.

"Hello," I say, my voice quiet.

There's no answer, but there never is.

"I know it's late already, but I wish the snow had waited," I continue, knowing the brownie is listening. "I'll miss walking in the gardens. I'm not sure how much longer I can take being trapped here."

The footsteps fade away, but it's not until they are gone completely that I turn. A teapot sits on the table, and fragrant steam rises from its spout. Two settings are carefully placed across from each other. In a few minutes, as I knew he would, Beau steps into the sitting room I've claimed as my own since our imprisonment.

He holds up a parchment invitation. "I've been summoned."

I've already poured his tea and am adding three cubes of sugar, just as he likes it—overwhelmingly sweet. "They didn't bother sending me one. I suppose they knew I'd be here."

Beau sets his invitation on the table and meets my gaze, studying me. I'm not sure what he sees, but he frowns. "You're always here."

"Where else am I to go?" I ask, lowering my gaze. "Wallow in my bed all day? Beg the kitchen brownie for a poisoned apple so I can sleep until I'm rescued?" I try to laugh, but the sound is hollow.

Instead of sitting, Beau takes several steps toward me, his eyes worried. "Are you so very miserable?"

Immediately, my gaze drops to my gown. I have dozens, all of them beautiful silks, velvets, and laces. New jewelry appears in the box in my room every few days—rubies, sapphires, emeralds. Diamonds.

The ogre decorates me like a pet. Like one of those tiny dogs Sabine carried around.

My stomach is always full. I want for nothing.

Except freedom. My family. Sunshine.

I sigh, working to push back these maudlin thoughts for

Beau's sake. For the first month, he paced like Puss, his temper a short fuse. Slowly, as he explored his family estate, his anger lessened. Though he's not at peace, he's resigned himself to our temporary fate.

At least the cat can come and go as he pleases. Puss is completely resistant to ogre magic. I've begged him to send word to my brothers, to Kerrick at least, but he insists we'll defeat the ogre on our own.

Lately, I almost think he knows how to accomplish it, too. There's a look in his sharp green eyes that betrays him, a smugness. But he's withholding the information, just another part of his insensible feline agenda.

Of course, Puss seems to be happy here. This is the life he wanted after all, even if it's not exactly how he planned it.

Startling me, Beau brushes his knuckles against my cheek. "Etta?"

Distracted by the soft press of his hand, I realize I never answered him. "No, I'm not miserable. I'm...restless."

Beau nods. He begins to lower his hand, and then he hesitates. Instead of moving away, he continues to trail his knuckles down my cheek, toward my jaw. As if it pains him, he again meets my eyes. His voice so soft I almost don't hear him, he says, "Would you hate me if I told you there are moments I'm glad this happened?"

My breath catches and everything fades around us. "Why?"

He shifts forward and swallows. Then, suddenly, he smiles and sits back, clearing his throat. "I feel as if I've reclaimed a piece of my father."

I sink into my seat, carefully avoiding his gaze. What started as flutters and warmth has grown into something far more complicated. I've been careful to hide it, but when he looks at me like that, I think that maybe, he might possibly...

Instead of sitting, Beau walks to the window. "He let you open the drapes."

"He does now," I say, stirring my own tea. "But they close as soon as I leave the room."

When we first arrived, the drapes would close the moment I turned away. And yet, for some reason, I never stopped trying.

The ogre is a conundrum. He's not happy, not even with all that he has stolen for himself, but he can be benevolent in his own way. He maintains his human form, more for my comfort than his own. Every night, he insists we join him for dinner—and every night, he and Beau quarrel. Eventually, Ettiene will heave a platter across the room and stalk to his quarters, leaving us and his plethora of dwarves in stunned silence.

You'd think we'd grow used to his tempers.

We drink our brownie-supplied tea, and then Beau leaves to find Puss. The cat has disappeared again. I'm not sure he's even at the estate right now.

Bored, I walk through the halls, opening curtains, leaving the rooms, and then peering back in to see if they've closed behind me. They have. I've spent most of my days like this, obsessed with light.

Tired with the ogre's obstinacy, I don a cloak and step into the gardens. The snow crunches under my feet, and I take in a deep breath of frozen fresh air. I make my way toward the back of the gardens, closest to the woods, where there are fewer guards and dwarves. Even the fairies are absent, probably warm in their tiny homes, wherever those may be.

I pause near a locked gate, resting my gloved hand on the iron bars, and peer into the forest. Even if I had the key, I couldn't pass. I turn, rest my back against the gate, and lower my hood. Soft, crystalline flakes drift downward, and I close my eyes, letting them fall on my face and eyelashes.

"The master has sent me to inform you that you'll be late for dinner if you don't head back in now," a dwarf says from not far away.

So much for being alone.

With my eyes still closed, I thank him and wait for him to leave. When he does, I linger a few more minutes, studying bare branches and looking for winter birds. Though the hem of my gown is wet, I don't bother changing for dinner. I hang the cloak on a peg near the door—it will find its way back to my room—and go to the dining hall.

"You're late, Etta," Ettiene says from his usual spot at the head of the table.

Beau sits a few seats down, on his right. As if he and the ogre have already been arguing, he looks irritated.

I don't bother to apologize—who apologizes to their jailer, after all?—and find my seat, which is directly across from Beau.

The mood of the evening is particularly tense, and it doesn't help when Puss leaps on the table, opposite the ogre in an obvious challenge.

"Remove the cat," Ettiene says to a human guard.

The man eyes Puss as he approaches. The last man who was ordered to "remove" Puss suffered from several painful, angry red scratches across his face. This guard doesn't take the risk of grabbing the cat, but instead tries to shoo him away.

Puss, irritated, purposely winds through the table settings, knocking over wine bottles and a saucière.

"Enough," I say, growing weary of the display. I pick up the cat and pull him onto my lap. Puss struggles to get away, but he soon quiets, grumbling softly to himself.

With the contrary cat in my arms, I gladly excuse myself from the dinner before dessert is served.

I drop Puss as soon as the doors close behind us.

"I've found a way for you to escape," he says without a preamble.

Freezing, I turn toward him. "What do you mean?"

He passes me, striding toward my quarters. If I want to hear what he has to say, I'll have to follow him. We wind through the halls, and the cat doesn't speak until we reach my room.

"I believe that if you're holding me, you can pass through the ogre's boundary."

Sitting on the bed, I say, "That's ridiculous."

"Is it?" Puss joins me and stretches out on his favorite spot on the end. "Not even worth trying?"

"How will leaving help Beau get his family home back?"

Puss yawns. "It won't. But it will allow you to go back to Kerrick. Marry the prince, leave this behind."

Irritated, I stand. "I promised I would help Beau. I won't leave until we've defeated the ogre." I look over my shoulder. "And I won't desert all the creatures trapped here, either."

"Fine," the cat says, closing his eyes. "Have it your way. But don't you think that if the boy wanted you, he'd have made his intentions clear by now?"

Slowly, I turn back. The cat opens one eye, scrunches his nose, and then lifts his head. "What is that look?"

What if Beau doesn't know how *I* feel about him? What if I haven't made myself clear? Perhaps I'm the one who needs to be brave. And if it ends badly, if Beau hates me for what I'm about to do, then I will try to leave with Puss.

"Where are you going?" Puss demands as I march out the door.

"To see Beau."

CHAPTER 37

Beau

THE OGRE IS BORED, VICIOUS, AND HE TAKES GREAT
amusement in tormenting me about my imprisonment.

"I'm surprised you haven't tried harder to save her," he
says after Etta leaves with Puss squirming in her arms.
"You're in love with her, aren't you?"

I pull my eyes away from the door, not wanting him to
sense how much I wish I could help Etta escape. I'd do
anything just to free her from this elaborate cage.

Even if letting her go would nearly kill me at this point.

"Why do you keep her?" I ask. "Why not set her free? She
means nothing to you. We both know it's me you want."

Now that Etta's gone, the ogre drops the mirage,
changing his form back to his true self.

"She's seen me and can never leave." He offers me a repul-
sive, toothy smile which makes my dinner churn in my stomach. "Besides, she's a nice addition to my collection, don't
you think?"

I stand, too angry to trust myself further and stalk to the
door. When I open the latch, the door sticks, not by lock but
by magic.

Seething, I wait for the ogre to free me.

"Is that any way to thank your host for the delicious meal?" he asks, laughing.

If I were to take a right hook to the guard to my left, could I relieve him of his sword before the others attacked? I'd have to be quick. The dwarves pack quite a punch, as I found out the first time I attempted to kill the ogre at dinner. And the second.

And the third.

"I wouldn't try it," the ogre says, reading my hesitance correctly. "Now. Let's remember our manners, and I'll let you go."

"Thank you for dinner," I say through gritted teeth.

"You can do better than that."

I stretch my head to the side, trying to relieve a kink in my neck. Still looking at the wooden door, I say, "Thank you, Monsieur Ettiene, for your hospitality. As always, we are ever so grateful."

The door swings open, hitting my chin when I don't step back fast enough.

"There," the ogre says, a smile in his voice. "Was that so difficult?"

Slamming the door behind me, I leave the dining hall, rubbing my jaw. When I reach my room, I find the usual bouquet on my bedside table. Each day it's changed out for a new one, and each day there are instructions to give the flowers to Etta.

The romantic kitchen brownie is a troublesome matchmaker.

Why don't they realize I don't deserve her? That I walked Etta into this mess, and I can't find a way to get her out. Thoughts of defeating the ogre and winning my family's land back are gone. The ogre's too powerful, and I am only one man.

As I do every day, I push the drapes aside, unlatch the window, and toss the flowers out.

I was selfish today, almost told Etta how I feel about her. It's getting more difficult, especially when we are each other's only allies besides Puss.

I will have to be more vigilant.

I'm rubbing my temples when a knock sounds at the door. I'm about to ask who it is when the door swings open and Etta strides into my room.

Her cheeks are flushed, and she looks like a woman on a mission.

"Beau, I…" she begins and then trails off, losing the nerve that was propelling her forward. Then she meets my eyes and takes a deep breath.

Just as I find myself smiling, wondering what this strange fit is about, she throws her arms around my neck. Too startled to think clearly, I stare at her, noticing for the first time the gold in her eyes. The smell of the flowers I just dumped out the window lingers in the air, mingling with the faint scent of the floral soap she uses in her hair.

Without another word, she kisses me.

CHAPTER 38

Beau goes statue-still, completely stunned and unresponsive.

What have I done?

How does one extract themselves from this position? Do I simply pull away, walk out the door? Pretend it never happened? Make an excuse?

And what kind of excuse is there? The dwarves put me up to it? The ogre enchanted me?

All these thoughts go through my head in a matter of seconds.

I pull back abruptly and remove my arms from his neck. "I'm sorry—"

Before I have the words out, Beau grabs my wrist and gently, but firmly, yanks me back. "Etta, *wait.*"

My heart thrums like fairy wings, making me light-headed. Embarrassed, overcome, I glance about the room, planning my escape.

"I thought," I stammer, feeling ridiculous. "I mean, I hoped...I was foolish. I apologize—"

When I try to yank away, Beau releases me only to grasp

my waist and pull me toward him. He's so close, I can hear his breath, feel each rise and fall of his chest. His eyelashes are dark and long, and they frame questioning eyes.

My mouth suddenly goes dry, and as I swallow, his gaze drops to my lips.

"Because of this time with you," he says quietly. "That's what I wanted to say earlier. Sometimes I'm glad this happened...*because I've spent this time with you.*"

We come together, no hesitation this time. We meet like the confluence of two rivers, forceful, with purpose. Too many months of veiled longing makes me throw caution to the wind.

My fingers delve into the soft, short hair at the nape of his neck. At the same time, he runs his hands up my torso to my back, pulling me closer still.

Here, in the bleakness that is the ogre's domain, Beau is light.

Slower now, softer, Beau trails soft kisses down my jaw then returns to my lips, deepening the kiss. My knees weaken.

I could stay like this forever, forget time altogether—if it weren't for a disgruntled mew behind us. We freeze, wrapped in each other's arms, and turn toward the small, furry intruder.

"Go to bed, Etta. I need to speak with the boy."

"No," I say, tired of taking orders from the cat.

Puss flicks his tail and narrows his eyes.

"It's late," Beau murmurs near my ear.

Turning toward him, I shoot him a questioning look.

In response, Beau ignores Puss and presses a soft kiss against my lips. "I'll see you in the morning."

Slowly, I extract myself from Beau's embrace. With one last disdainful look at my cat, I sweep down the hall and into my room.

CHAPTER 39

Beau

"I'VE FOUND A WAY FOR ETTA TO ESCAPE," PUSS SAYS THE moment Etta closes the door.

A heaviness settles in my stomach at his words, and I step back and sink into the chair behind me. "How?"

My mind wanders as he explains. It seems I have a choice. I can leave as well, go back to my life, leave the ogre be.

Or I can stay, find a way to honor the promise I made to my father on his deathbed.

"Etta's in danger here," Puss says finally. "The ogre is enchanted with her now. What will he do when that changes? What if one of these days he realizes that hurting her would be a new form of torture for you?"

I sink my head into my hands, wanting to argue, but there are no words. As usual, Puss is right.

"Once she's safe, I'll come back," Puss finishes.

The cat's promise startles me from my thoughts. "Why would you do that?"

He narrows his eyes. "Because I believe I know how to defeat the ogre. But it's dangerous, and I won't attempt it if

189

she's here. Send Etta away. If you truly love her, you'll make the hard decision."

"All right," I finally say, hating myself.

But no matter what comes to pass, I want Etta free and safe. The thought keeping her trapped here when I have the power to help her escape—I can't do it. I can't keep her here selfishly, not just because she's the only thing making this life bearable.

I pause outside Etta's door, preparing myself for this confrontation. After several moments, I knock.

"Who is it?" Etta calls after several moments, sounding half asleep.

She opens the door only moments after I call to her. Immediately, she knows something is wrong. Her sleepy smile fades when she takes in my grim expression.

"What is it?" she asks, her voice low.

I look away and swallow. "You need to go with Puss."

"He told you." Her voice is low and accusing.

She takes a step back as if I struck her, and my gut twists. I angle my head, avoiding her eyes.

"No," she finally says.

I look back. "Etta, this place is dangerous. You're not safe here."

Etta turns and stalks across the room. "I'm not leaving."

Shutting the door behind me, wincing when the wood closes with a loud thud in the quiet hours of night, I follow her. "You don't have a choice. I won't keep you here—not when you can be free."

Crossing her arms, she shakes her head. "It's not your decision to make."

I want to reach out for her, want to run away with her

and be done with this place. But I can't do that, not when I gave my father my word. I know her too well now; there's only one reason she'll leave. Though I might as well stab her in the heart. Heaven knows I'll be doing it to myself as well.

"You should go back to Kerrick," I say, looking at the canopy above her bed. I hear my voice, hear how cold it sounds.

She's silent for so long, I have to look back at her. She stands still, a disbelieving look in her eyes.

"Even if I somehow find a way to vanquish the ogre...we wouldn't work," I say. "You have a life here. I have a life at sea."

"I know what you're doing."

I finally meet her eyes, pin her with my gaze. "Then let me do it." I close the distance between us and grasp her shoulders. "You said you wanted the poisoned apple? Skip that step and let me save you."

Looking slightly bitter, she shakes her head. "What's the point if you're still here?"

After taking a deep breath, I run my fingers through her hair. "Go to your prince, Etta. That was your story before I interfered. You were supposed to be with him."

"How could you possibly know that?"

I attempt a smile, but I'm afraid it's grim. "That's the way these things work."

"But I want *you*."

Her words cut me to my core, and I close my eyes. This being noble bit can go to oblivion.

"And I love you, Etta. I do. So much, I'd rather rip out my heart and send you away with it than keep you here."

CHAPTER 40

As I stand here, listening to the agony in Beau's voice, feeling my heart shatter in my chest, I realize what I have to do.

I will save Beau, help him keep his promise to his father—even if it means forfeiting my own life, living the rest of my days in the bottom of the king's dungeons.

And I will have to leave to do it.

Beau's still speaking, telling me why he has no choice but to send me away.

Leaning forward to cut him off, I press my lips against his and murmur, "I'll go."

Obviously surprised, he pauses and threads his hands through my hair. Disbelief and concern shows in his eyes. "You will?"

I nod and slide my hands up his chest. "But I don't want to speak of it now."

He closes his eyes and rests his forehead against mine, wrapping his arms around my back, holding me secure. I return his embrace, locking him close, knowing our time is short.

"THIS WILL NEVER WORK, PUSS," I SAY, PEERING OUT THE GATE that leads to the forest. "It's too simple."

It's early dawn, and the sun hasn't yet crested the horizon. We haven't tried to leave again, not since the ogre first trapped us here, and we certainly can't try to walk out over the drawbridge.

I hold a satchel of hard cheese, bread, and dried fruits in my hand. Somehow, the uncanny kitchen brownie knew what we were plotting.

"Sometimes the most effective solutions are the simplest," Puss says, undeterred by my doubt.

Turning to Beau, I twist the satchel in my hands. "What will Ettiene do to you when he finds me gone?"

Beau shrugs. "It doesn't matter what the ogre will do."

"It does matter." Worry continues to build, and now it's near suffocating. "Come with me. There's no reason for you to stay."

As I knew he would, he shakes his head. "This is something I have to do."

Nodding, I kiss him one last time. "I'll miss you."

"As soon as I defeat the ogre," Beau promises. "I will find you."

Unless I find him first.

Beau slides the stolen key into the lock and swings the gate open. The forest waits, calm and quiet, the snow undisturbed.

With one last long glance, I scoop Puss into my arms. Ready to meet the barrier, I step through the gate…and pass through.

"That's ridiculous," I scoff, irritated that it was so simple.

As Puss predicted, his resistance enveloped me simply because I was holding him.

Curious if I will be blocked from this side, I drop the cat and stretch my hand out for Beau. My fingers hit an invisible barrier, and I let my hand drift down to my side.

"This isn't goodbye," I insist.

Beau nods, but his eyes betray him. He's not sure.

"I'M LEAVING YOU NOW," PUSS SAYS. "YOU'LL BE FINE from here."

The cottages of Glenridge are in the distance, welcoming me home. I found a farmer to give me a ride most of the way, but we've trudged the last few miles through the snow. My hands are frozen, and my feet are numb.

I glance at the cat. "Where are you going?"

"Back to the Carabas estate."

Leaning down, I scoop up Puss. His fur is dusted with snow, and his tiny paws are frigid. "What are you plotting?"

"I'm going to slay the ogre."

"*You* are?"

He twists his body, looking up at me with disdain. "You don't have to look so doubtful."

"I'm going to the king," I tell him. "I'm going to tell him everything. He'll send help."

Puss hisses and leaps from my arms. "You'll do no such thing—not yet."

"I've already decided, Puss."

"Give me time," he says. "If we're not back by the end of the second week in spring, then you may speak with His Majesty."

Sighing, I turn toward the snow-covered boughs of the nearby forest. Though it's still cold, water drips from the icicles clinging to the limbs, making tiny tunnels in the snow at the base of the trees. Spring is not so very far off.

"All right," I agree. "But if you haven't returned…"

He nods, and then, without any further goodbyes, runs back the way we came. I watch him go, waiting until his furry figure disappears over a hill. After he's gone, I continue on through the town, heading toward the mill.

If I thought I received odd looks when I first donned my hunting outfit, it's nothing like the attention my gown is getting after my season-long absence.

I wave to the tailor's wife, and she stares at me with wide eyes.

"Etta!" she says, so stunned that she comes to a complete stop halfway in the street. "We thought…"

Judging from how pale she's gone, they must have thought the worst. Her eyes travel down my gown, and her jaw goes slack.

"I'm fine," I assure her, "but I have to see my brothers."

Her face softens. "Thomas is away."

"Is he still in Rynvale?"

She purses her lips. "No, Etta. He's gone to the coast to sell his figurines to merchants."

Her news takes me by surprise. I never thought Thomas would leave, never imagined him truly gone.

"And Eugene?"

"He and Sarah-Anne wed a month ago."

My brother married while I was away. My throat tightens. What else has changed while I've been imprisoned in the Carabas estate?

I say my goodbyes and hurry down the ice-covered lane to the mill. Smoke rises from the chimney, and a newly built barn stands behind the mill. For the first time in years, black and white cows stand in the pasture.

The buildings look better as well.

Suddenly and inexplicably nervous, I stand on the threshold and knock.

After several moments, Sarah-Anne opens the door. Her eyes go wide when she finds me shivering on the step. Eugene appears behind her, and he narrows his eyes, shocked. It isn't until an icicle drips a very cold drop of water down my neck that the two find their voices and usher me inside.

"What happened to you?" Eugene demands. "Where have you been?"

"Did you run away with that chocolatier?" Sarah-Anne asks, recovering quickly. "That's what everyone's said. It's been quite the scandal. You and Beau disappeared together, and now…" She motions her hand toward my gown.

I sit at the familiar, worn table and tell them my story, minus the part Puss played in it. It's not easy to leave the cat out of the tale, but I manage well enough.

At the end, the two stare at me like they don't quite believe it.

"If you'll let me stay the night," I say, "tomorrow I'll go to Rynvale and speak with Kerrick."

Sarah-Anne rests her chin on her hand. "*Prince* Kerrick."

I nod.

"And Beau is still there, in his family's home, imprisoned by an ogre?" Eugene asks, incredulous.

"For now."

"You are more than welcome here," Sarah-Anne says. "We haven't touched the loft."

"Thank you," I say, setting my hand on hers to show how grateful I am. "But only for the night."

This isn't my home anymore.

"The mill looks better," I say.

Eugene and Sarah-Anne exchange a look.

"What is it?"

Uncomfortable, Eugene looks at the table. "Not long after you disappeared with Beau, right after we bought the cows,

Broussard demanded half the proceeds from this year's harvest."

"We thought he was going to wait until next year to collect," Sarah-Anne adds. "But he has the deed, so there was little we could do."

My heart aches for my brother, but I did warn them. Though it still feels as if this is my fault. If I'd married Broussard...but no. I couldn't bear to chain myself to a man who loves money as much as he does.

"We're doing well enough," Eugene assures me, but I'm not certain he's being altogether truthful.

After we speak for several more hours, I climb the ladder. At the top, I stare at the faded, patched quilt that covers my pallet. My night shift is folded on the table where I left it months ago, but it's dusty from sitting for so long. I run my hand over the threadbare fabric, remembering what my life was like until recently. So much has changed.

Missing Beau so much my heart aches, I blow out the candle.

CHAPTER 41

Beau

"Tell me how she escaped!" The ogre paces back and forth, livid.

I hang from the dungeon walls, my wrists chained. It took two men and three dwarves to capture me. For that, I'm proud. My face throbs from where the monster punched me, and it's swollen so badly, I can't see out of my right eye.

Despite the pain I'm in, my only thoughts remain on Etta and how glad I am she's gone.

The ogre turns back, his beady eyes narrowed in anger. "Tell me now, and I may show mercy on her—because I will find her, Carabas. I'll send men out all through this kingdom and the next, looking for her. And when I do bring her back, you and she will both wish she were dead."

An involuntary chill passes through me. Please let her have gone back to the king, let her be safe in the palace.

CHAPTER 42

I WAIT IN LINE BEHIND A TALL, LEAN PIG FARMER WHO quarrels with a short, stout sheep farmer. I had assumed, with it being the middle of winter, that there would be fewer people seeking an audience with the king. I was wrong.

Behind me, a woman holds a crying baby. The newborn's mewling cries sound like the yowls of a cat, and several times I almost turn around to make sure it is, in fact, a child. When I do glance back, I find the woman isn't much older than I am. She wears a desperate, world-weary sort of look. She meets my eyes and gives me a tired, apologetic sort of smile as she rubs the baby's back.

I return it and turn back toward the front, listening to the two farmers argue over the price of bacon versus wool. Apparently, according to the sheep farmer, he has been cheated out of two copper coins.

We near the front, and the baby cries again, hiccupping now that it's so upset. The noise fades to the background, because there, in front of me, Kerrick stands with his father.

He looks as handsome as I remember, his hair slightly

darker now in the winter months. After having been through this all morning, he seems restless.

As I watch him, I grow nervous. For one small moment, I wonder if he's forgotten about me. Could such a thing happen in one short season?

"Go ahead," I say, motioning the woman forward, not wanting to speak with the king and his son over the baby's desperate cries. Besides, the woman's situation is apparently more urgent than mine.

After King Deloge sorts out the bacon/wool situation, the woman goes forward, bowing low with the baby in her arms. Over the child's cries, she quickly explains that her husband passed away in the autumn and she's seeking employment. The king waves a steward over, instructing them to take the woman to the kitchens for food for her and milk for the child, and then find her a suitable position.

The woman falls to her knees, tears streaming down her face as she thanks His Majesty, and both the king and Kerrick watch as she hurries after the guard.

Another steward, this one recognizing me, ushers me forward.

"You shouldn't have waited, my lady," he says, appalled that I'd stand here with the commoners.

As one, the king and Kerrick turn their attention toward me, expecting another struggling peasant, no doubt. Even as the king's face breaks into a wide smile, Kerrick goes very still.

I hold up a bag, not the one I lost that autumn day by the stream, but another from the tailor, and bow low. "I have brought you a gift, Your Majesty."

"Suzette!" the king exclaims, rising from his throne and coming toward me. "What a pleasure it is to see you, my dear." He takes my offered bag. As he hands it off to the steward who's still at my side, he peers inside. "Snow rabbits!

You are a clever huntress. And here I thought it was your men trapping the animals for you."

"No, Sire," I say, unable to hide my smile.

Once free of the bag, the king clutches my hands in his own. "My huntsman has just informed me there is to be a blizzard coming in from the north. I must insist you stay with us."

Before I answer, I glance at Kerrick. He looks pensive, uneasy. Not for me, as before, but rather of me. Unsure how to read his expression, I turn back to the king. "I am grateful for your hospitality."

"Where is your man?" the king asks, and I can only assume he's speaking of Beau.

For a moment, I debate telling him with the hopes that he will forgive my deception long enough to gather his great armies and lay siege on the ogre. Just when the words are on the tip of my tongue, I remember my promise to Puss.

"Tending to Carabas affairs," I say instead.

The king nods and waves his son forward. "Kerrick, won't you show the marquise to her room? I'm sure she's exhausted after her long journey."

"And hunting trip," Kerrick adds. For the first time, he lets a small smile slip through.

I return the smile, relieved. Glancing around, I ask, "How is Sabine?"

Kerrick's smile dims. "Well. Yes—she's well. And home, temporarily." Then clearing his throat, he offers his arm. "Shall we?"

He escorts me from the throne room. When we are away and quite alone, he releases me. His eyes take in my gown, the same I traveled home in yesterday, and he frowns in a quizzical sort of way. "Did you take care of whatever it was Beau needed your help with?"

I shake my head. "No. He is still there, tending to it just as I told your father."

His bright eyes take me in. "I was beginning to think I dreamt you up. You walked into my life so suddenly, and then you left the same way."

I wait for my heart to stir, wonder if butterflies will take wing. But my heart and my stomach stay still. The only thing I feel when I look at him is a warm affection very similar in nature to how I feel about Eugene or Thomas. I don't love Kerrick. I suspect I never did, not in a lasting, real sort of way.

Not in the way I've come to love Beau.

"Sabine and I have announced our engagement," Kerrick blurts out suddenly.

I blink, startled more by the delivery than the announcement itself. "Well...congratulations."

"You left me so abruptly," he says quickly—as if he must explain. "And you seemed so certain that we weren't—"

Setting my hand on his arm, I cut him off. Hoping the sincerity of my words shines through, I say, "Sabine will be a lovely queen."

He runs a hand through his thick, blond hair. "But now you're here, and I..."

I shake my head, silencing him. "You made the right decision."

Looking torn, he lets his hand fall to his side. "Did I, Etta?"

"You did."

"I'm not sure I love her." The prince walks toward a window, one that's open to the day and letting in lots of muted winter sunlight, and stares out at his white kingdom. "Not like I thought, once, that I was in love with you."

I join him at the window. "What we had was beautiful, bright...fleeting. But it wasn't a forever sort of love."

Kerrick looks over, confirming that his heart is in the same place. "No matter, I'm glad you're back, Etta. Tell me how you've been."

We find a soft, out of the way nook, and I tell him of Beau and the ogre. I even tell him Puss's part in the whole thing. He looks astounded, doubtful, but he doesn't question me.

"We will send men," Kerrick promises as soon as I'm finished, "at exactly the second week of spring."

"Thank you, Kerrick. You truly are a good friend." When he looks as if he's doubting himself again, I say, "Now tell me of Sabine's plans for your wedding."

CHAPTER 43

Beau

AN ANGRY HISS ECHOES IN MY SMALL, DARK CELL, AND I JERK awake. A torch was left burning outside the bars, but it must have gone out sometime in the night. Only a dim glow comes from above the stairway just outside the cell. Half asleep, I scan the room.

"Puss?" I whisper when I see a small, furry creature passing between the bars.

"Well, this is a fine mess," his familiar voice says as he pauses in front of me. "We'll have to wait until he releases you."

"Releases me?" I half croak, half laugh. "I wouldn't count on that."

A small overturned crate sits forgotten in the corner. The cat shoves it over to me with his head, and I stumble onto it, eager to take the weight off my arms. My shoulders are stiff and numb. Agonizing pain shoots through them when I move, and I groan out loud. I've only been here since this afternoon, but it's been far too long in my opinion.

When Etta didn't come to dinner last night, I stayed silent. The ogre assumed she was feeling ill and left me be.

But by this afternoon, when his eyes and ears in the castle reported no one had seen her, he flew into a rage.

"He will release you," the cat says, his voice full of certainty. "He keeps you for entertainment, as someone to constantly needle. Throwing you in here brought him temporary joy, but now he has no one to torment. I give it two days, tops."

I growl at the thought of hanging here for two more days. Surely my arms will fall off. "I hope you're right, cat."

"Yes, well. I may have overheard him speaking of it as well. I'll be back tomorrow if you're still here," Puss promises.

"Wait," I say, but he's already slipped through the bars, and his shadowy form disappears up the stairs.

Somehow I make it through the rest of the night. Sleep comes in blissful intervals, bringing with it sweet relief from the all-consuming ache in my arms, but I'm never unconscious long. When I do drift, my dreams are a chaotic jumble of memories and harsh colors.

When the sun finally rises high enough for the light to come from the windows above the stairs, I'm more exhausted than I was to begin with. My mouth is dry, and my throat is sore. Somehow I doze again. This time, I'm woken by the ogre's harsh voice coming from the top of the stairs. I take a deep breath, mentally preparing myself for the pain I'm about to self-inflict, and kick the crate away.

If the ogre were to see the wooden box, he'd not only question how it got here, but punish me further for its very existence.

The crate shifts, and I fall abruptly. The weight of my body jerks against my restrained wrists. Metal cuffs dig into my skin, and the combination of raw pain plus the lack of food makes my stomach heave.

"Have a pleasant evening?" the ogre asks when he comes

into view. Apparently, I look as close to death as I feel because a wide, satisfied smile spreads across his face, showing off his tusk-like teeth. "I think he's had enough for now. Let him down."

A dour-looking human guard rushes forward, fumbling with his keys, and releases me. Showing the barest amount of kindness, he grasps me under my arm before he releases the first cuff, which keeps me from falling farther and potentially dislocating my other shoulder.

Still, an agonized cry slips past my lips as my arm is released. The expected relief is more like a hot-burning fire, all consuming. My stomach rolls again, but since it's thankfully empty, I don't further humiliate myself in front of the beast.

When the last cuff is opened, I fall to the ground in a heap. My eyes sting; my hands are numb and useless.

"Bring him along," the ogre says, already turning up the stairs. The guard drags me to an awkward standing position, and I stumble after them. The two twist and turn through the halls, and, eventually, I find myself in front of the room that had been given to me when we first arrived.

The ogre shoves me inside. "A maid will bring up a bath. I expect you at breakfast."

The door slams behind me, and I'm left exhausted, sore, and more than a little bewildered.

CHAPTER 44

Etta

THE FIRST DAY OF SPRING IS HERALDED IN BY A SNOWSTORM. A blizzard did, indeed, hit Rynvale the night I arrived in the palace, and another followed on its heels. As the new season approached, the snow became heavier, wetter, and the storms more violent.

Every night at dinner His Majesty insisted I stay a little longer. With nowhere to go, I was only too happy to agree.

Now, as I pace my beautiful, light blue room, I grow eager to leave. I had expected Puss back by now. Surely if his grand plan had gone as expected, the ogre should be vanquished.

But there is no sign of Beau or my cat.

Several more days pass, and finally, on the fifth day of spring, the sun shines. By the ninth day, the snow begins to melt, and by the thirteenth day, dirty bits of trampled ice cling to the shadows only. The roads leading from Rynvale are mud. The days are still cold enough that a cloak is needed to venture outside, and only the hardiest of the spring flora has begun to grow.

Tonight, I shall speak with the king about the ogre.

Kerrick no longer seems nervous the king will fly into a rage and lock me in the stocks. Apparently, because I'm no longer a contender for Kerrick's hand, my lineage means little.

I adjust my gown, this one commissioned for me by the king when he noticed I only had the one I arrived in, and make my way to the king's dining hall. I know my way around the palace now, know the shortcuts through the servant's quarters and the seldom-used halls.

To my great surprise, when I pass through the doors, I find Sabine sitting on Kerrick's right, smiling as she feeds her tiny, white puff of a dog bits of roasted goose.

The princess looks up when I step into the room. She stands so abruptly; the little dog almost falls from her lap. At the last possible moment, she snatches the tiny creature and clutches it to her chest. A gossamer vision in white, Sabine sweeps from the table and pulls me into an embrace.

Between us, her little dog squirms, desperate for air.

"Hello, Sabine," I manage to say with my mouth pressed against her hair.

She pulls back and studies me. "It's so good to see you, Suzette!"

"Congratulations on your upcoming wedding."

Sabine positively beams and loops my arm through hers, dragging me to the empty seat at her side. Once there, she finally lowers her dog to the ground and the poor thing cowers at her feet, glad to be free but unsure what to do with himself now that he is.

"It will be a June wedding," Sabine begins, "because that is when the roses are the most fragrant…"

She continues on, and I smile and nod, so bemused with her exuberance that I almost forget my purpose for this evening. Kerrick listens to Sabine, an indulgent half-smile playing on his lips, and he gives opinions only when he's asked. The princess beams at him, touching him often, and I am content their marriage will be a happy one.

Kerrick catches my eye, and I smile. Thoughtful, he nods, almost reading my mind.

Eventually, now that we've discussed flowers, silks, composers, and orchestras, there is a lull in the conversation.

I clear my throat, nervous this will go badly. It's a small gathering, only King Deloge, Kerrick, Sabine, and the princess's matron aunt who traveled with her, but it's still terrifying. Kerrick, realizing my purpose while dabbing his mouth with his napkin, lowers the linen to his lap, looking grim.

"Suzette," he says, "I think it would be best if I were to explain."

Gulping, somewhat relieved, I nod. Kerrick begins to explain the events of last spring, omitting the romantic bits for Sabine's benefit. The king's expression becomes incredulous as his son goes on, and I can't imagine what he would do if anyone had known how my cat was involved.

"So Beau, the true Marquis of Carabas, is being held hostage in his own estate, a prisoner of an ogre who has cast a spell on not only him, but our people as well," Kerrick finishes.

His Majesty takes several moments, nodding to himself, and then meets my eyes. "You lied to me, Suzette."

Blinking quickly, there is nothing I can do but admit that I did.

He crosses his arms and leans back against his chair. "But you were, in fact, the one who sent me the gifts?"

"Yes, Your Majesty," I say, lowering my eyes.

"Kerrick, why don't you show Lady Julia and Sabine the paintings your mother did?"

The prince rises, looking reluctant to leave. Before Sabine

steps from her chair, she squeezes my hand. The pair goes, taking Sabine's wide-eyed aunt with them. I'm sure she hadn't expected this kind of excitement.

Once they are gone, and the doors have shut behind them, the king turns back to me. I feel tiny, insignificant, and I await my punishment, hoping with all my heart he will take pity on Beau and send him aid.

"I already knew," the king says finally.

It's the last thing I expect him to say, and I gape at him.

"Well, not everything." He smiles, his expression kind, apparently finding amusement in the fact that he has taken me off guard. "But I remembered you from the first day you brought the rabbits, and then I overheard you and Kerrick speaking in the garden the day after we found you like a mermaid in the creek. I knew you were not of the Carabas family, for since the moment you first arrived, I've had a nagging suspicion that their name was one I should remember."

"Your Majesty?"

He continues, "I looked them up in the book of records, found that they are the family who resides just on the other side of my border to the south. And then it all came back to me, though what their fate was, I couldn't say. Since they reside outside my kingdom, I wasn't aware of their affairs." He grimaces. "An ogre? Nasty business."

I study my hands in my lap, unsure what to say.

"I'll inform my captain of the guard, and we will be off in the morning. You'll have to come with us, of course. I have no idea how to get there."

Startled, I jerk my head up and find him in good humor. "You'll help?"

The king leans forward. "Of course I will."

Blinking, I look down again. "I'm sorry. So truly sorry..." I bite my lip to hold back humiliated tears.

"I know you are. And you are forgiven." He pushes away from the table, comes to me, offering me his hand, and smiles benevolently. "For you see, I am so very fond of wild game, and you, dear girl, have brought me only the best."

CHAPTER 45

Beau

"Do you remember what you have to do?" Puss asks for the what seems like the hundredth time. He's sitting atop my doublet, getting cat hair all over the velvet brocade.

Not that I care about the clothing, but I don't care for the fur in my food, which is where it always seems to end up.

I shoo him off my bed. "Yes, yes."

Disgruntled, Puss jumps down. Before he slips out the door, he looks back over his shoulder. "This is our one chance. Do not botch it up."

The faith he has in me is humbling.

After the cat is gone, I pull on the doublet. Tonight's the night. If all goes as planned, we will be free of the ogre, and I will be master of this estate.

And tomorrow I will find Etta and ask her to marry me. I'll live here, give up the sea if I have to. Whatever she wants, I will do.

But first, the ogre.

The weeks since my imprisonment have been trying. The creature has been in a foul mood, irritable over the fact that his men have not tracked Etta down yet. I, personally, don't think they're trying very hard. I know I wouldn't, if I were them.

Before I leave the room, I tuck a palm-sized paper package on my nightstand table along with a note to my friend in the kitchens. In all this time, I've still never seen her. Since she's a brownie, I likely never will.

After my night hanging on the dungeon wall, she secreted muscle-relieving salves and pain-reducing herbs into my room. In fact, every evening I find something from her when I return from dinner—extra pastries, sweet rolls, and other things of that sort.

Hopefully she'll find the narcotic before the meal is over —hopefully she's more loyal to me than the ogre.

I don't look for Puss when I stride into the dining hall, don't risk giving his location away. He's to hide in the shadows of a potted plant in the corner, where he'll hopefully remain unnoticed throughout the meal.

As soon as I walk through the doors, I sense the ogre is in a particularly vile mood this evening. His dwarves and guards seem wary, and the mood is tense.

He turns his eyes on me as I take my seat. "Tonight you will tell me how the human girl escaped."

Every night he asks me this question, relieving my worry, letting me know he's yet to find Etta and question her himself. But something instinctual warns me that I must be careful how I allow it to play out tonight.

"You know your magic better than anyone else," I say just the same as always, not bothering to meet his eyes as I pull a roll from the platter in front of me. "How do you think she escaped?"

The ogre growls and stabs a dagger into the table next to his plate. The extreme outburst startles me, and I almost drop the roll.

The ogre doesn't bother with his human form any longer.

He never plays at pleasantries now that Etta isn't here to impress, but now he's especially hostile.

"Bring in the brownie," the ogre snarls to one of the dwarves.

The short, stout man blinks at his master in surprise. "Do you mean the kitchen brownie?"

The ogre narrows his eyes. "I wasn't aware we had more than one."

Swallowing, unsettled, the dwarf hurries away.

I go cold, pausing with my butter knife poised over my roll. Seeing my reaction, the ogre smiles for the first time this evening.

"Now that I have your attention," he says, folding his hands together on the table in an uncanny human-like gesture. "Tell me how the girl escaped."

Around me, the guards are very still. They seem to be holding their breaths, wondering how I will answer.

I'd like to know as well.

I choose to ignore the question as if he hadn't asked it. I bite into the bread, purposely avoiding his gaze, but I've noticed something very important.

He's not eating.

How is the narcotic powder Puss gave me to pass to the kitchen brownie supposed to work if the ogre hasn't touched his food? And has she even had a chance to find it? I was hoping she'd slip it into his pie, maybe sprinkle it into his dessert wine.

The thoughts are forgotten when the dwarf comes in, pulling with him a woman smaller than he is, hidden under a simple brown cloak. She whimpers, terrified of being seen by this many eyes. The ogre, showing no pity on her, drags her hood down.

She cringes, trying to hide her pale face with her hands, but it's to no avail because we've all seen her now.

The brownie resembles a dwarf, but softer, with more rounded features. Her cheeks are rosy and slightly wrinkled, and her eyes are bright, bright blue. I have no idea what age she may be as brownies can live for hundreds of years.

It's possible she haunted the kitchens while my father was but a boy.

The ogre yanks the dagger from the table and holds it to her throat. "You know how the girl escaped. Tell me."

She makes a soft noise, an obvious refusal, and the ogre pushes the blade closer. A small trickle of dark red blood trails down her neck, and anger builds in my core.

"Tell me!" he yells, making her tremble anew.

"Etta carried the cat," I snarl. "His immunity to your magic passed to her, and she stepped right through your ward."

For one moment, I think he may slit the poor creature's throat even though I've told him, but he tosses her away. A dwarven server runs forward, clutching the brownie in her arms. Without asking for permission, she ushers the tiny, trembling woman out the side door.

The ogre's eyes flash, and he turns toward the guard at his left. "The cat lurks somewhere in the castle. I want it found and gutted. I'll have it for breakfast tomorrow." He turns his attention back to me. "And then you can have the fur made into a muff—a gift for Etta for when she returns."

It takes everything in me to keep from glancing at the plant in the corner.

The guard leaves and an unnatural silence falls over the room.

Without the help of Puss's mind-addling poison to take away the ogre's inhibitions, I'm not sure I can pull this off. But I have no choice.

"It's good you surround yourself with guards and

dwarves, Ogre." I purposefully meet his eyes. "Because it seems you are not as powerful as you want people to believe."

The expressions that pass over the men's faces who stand along the wall would be comical if my death weren't imminent.

Slowly, deliberately, the ogre leans toward me. "What did you say?"

"I said it appears you hide behind your guards and dwarves, too weak to fight your own battles." I wait a moment before continuing. "For a shape-shifter, you're rather pathetic. After all, your greatest power is to change into a human. Not terribly impressive, really."

"Leave us," the ogre says to his men. Clenching his gruesome jaw, the ogre leans forward. "I can change into anything I please."

The guards look at me with something akin to pity as they filter out of the room, knowing that I've cheerfully, and foolishly, signed my death warrant.

"Perhaps," I shrug and then look at my plate as if bored. "What about a...lion? I don't believe you can change into something that mighty. Surely you wouldn't need this much protection if you could."

The speed in which he shifts nearly stops my heart. One moment I'm talking to him, the next a gigantic feline prowls over the long dining room table, batting plates aside and growling as he stalks toward me.

Scooting my chair back, properly terrified, I quickly say, "Apparently I was wrong."

The lion still appears as if he's going to attack.

"A lion is impressive, yes, but what about an elephant?" I continue. "Can you change into a beast that large? Surely not."

With a loud crack and flying wood, the table collapses as the lion morphs into a creature so gigantic, there is scarcely room for him. Dishes, settings, and candelabras fly this way and that.

The elephant holds a huge foot over me. "Are you impressed yet, Carabas?"

"Quite," I squeak and then clear my throat. "But, now that I think of it, it's only natural that a large creature such as yourself can change into other large creatures. Not that difficult, really."

Slowly, the ogre-elephant lowers his foot, looking as if he's about to gore me with his tusks.

Standing, hoping to put a little distance between me and the beast, I add, "But to change into something tiny, something insignificant—now that would be a feat."

"Like what, Carabas?" the ogre glares at me with foreign eyes. "A rabbit? A grouse?"

I shrug. "Certainly, but what about something as tiny as… a mouse? That would be quite impossible, would it not?"

And just like that, the elephant is gone, vanished before my very eyes. I frantically look for him in the broken plates, splintered table, and mess of molten wax on the floor. Before I even spot the rodent the ogre shifted into, Puss leaps into the middle of the mess, pouncing with outstretched paws and a greedy look in his bright green eyes.

A tiny gray tail disappears into the cat's mouth, and that is my very last glimpse of the ogre.

I stare at Puss with disbelief. The world slows, and the steady thrum of the grandfather clock in the corner is the only thing that tells me that time hasn't actually stopped.

"It worked," I say dumbly when I find my voice.

"Of course it worked," the cat scoffs, licking his chops in a very satisfied sort of way. He begins to lick his paw and proceeds to groom his face. "It was my idea."

WHEN I STEP INTO THE HALL, HUMANS AND DWARVES BOTH gape at me, obviously not expecting that I should be the one to return after the chaos they heard through the door.

I cross my arms and clear my throat, unnerved by their undivided attention.

Puss saunters past me, undaunted, and announces, "Open the drapes, clean the windows. Fill the vases and polish the good silver. Captain Gregory?"

An older guard who I'd never bothered to learn the name of snaps to attention, looking bewildered. "Yes…Cat?"

"Spread the word. The ogre has been vanquished and the Marquis of Carabas has returned."

As the growing crowd gasps at the cat's bold declaration, the guard blinks, his memory slowly filling in the blanks caused by the ogre's magic. He turns to me, eyes narrowed with disbelief, more concerned with my title than the talking. "My lord? I do not know you."

Puss glares at me, and I stand taller.

"I am Bradley Marchand's son—and your new marquis."

At my words, the men in attendance bow. The dwarves, of course, do not, but I do believe we've earned their admiration by defeating the monster holding them captive.

One steps forward. His dark brown eyes are nearly hidden under his massive black beard and mustache. "Congratulations on your victory, My Lord Carabas. After all this time, my kind shall be taking our leave. Our sincerest thanks." He clasps a hand over his heart and bows his head.

"Why did he keep you here…" I ask but trail off as I look through the newly opened windows and see dwarves and fairies already testing the wards and yelling with joy when they find they are able to cross the drawbridge.

The dwarf scowls. "He couldn't hold this much magic on his own. He captured creatures of magic—drained us to hold his spells—including the one that locked us here."

"He used your own magic to hold you prisoner?"

He nods. "Again, we are very grateful to you."

When the dwarf steps back, Puss growls at our audience. "What are you waiting for? Tonight we entertain a king!"

The remaining crowd of mostly humans snaps to attention, and they scurry off, all tending to the cat's commands.

"A king?" I ask Puss, incredulous.

He gives me a feline smile, already proud of himself. "What day is it, Beau?"

I shake my head, unable to follow his strange line of thought. "The third of April, I believe."

Satisfied, he says, "Etta is already on her way."

CHAPTER 46

"I've forgotten my gloves!" Sabine says, pushing past me as she rushes from the carriage. Her golden curls bounce in the sun as she calls back over her shoulder, "I'll only be a moment!"

I'm anxious, ready to begin our journey, and even though I'm fond of the princess, I'd rather leave her here.

"Tell me again why she's coming?" I ask Kerrick.

"Because she wants to see the countryside," the king answers instead.

I glance out the window at the soldiers on horseback, who are ready to accompany us to the ogre's gates. The plumes on their hats dance in the breeze, and their rapiers, secure in baldrics, glint at their sides. Each wear sashes of different colors, denoting their rank in His Majesty's army.

"You and she will stay safe in the carriage," the king assures me.

Still thinking it's foolish, I sit against the velvet upholstered seat and wait for the princess to return. Soon, Sabine rushes into the courtyard, today a vision in lavender silk and ivory lace. The footman helps her into the carriage, and she takes her place next to Kerrick, practically smothering him with the bountiful fabric of her skirts.

She smiles at me, obviously excited for the adventure, and daintily pulls on her gloves.

We finally begin our journey. It will take most of the day, and we're already getting a later start than I would like. At this rate, we'll reach the Carabas land well after dark.

By the time the sun sets, however, I realize I was wrong. We're still hours away, and Sabine's already yawning.

Much to my dismay, we stop at a grand castle belonging to Kerrick's cousin.

"We can't stop now!" I hiss to the prince as the rest of our party mingles with the nobles and their men.

Kerrick crosses his arms. "You had to know we wouldn't make it all in one day."

"Beau and I did," I insist.

"Yes, but you were traveling far lighter."

Glancing around the courtyard, my eyes wander over our ridiculously large party.

"Get some sleep," Kerrick says. "We'll be there tomorrow."

Though my room is opulent and my bed is downy, I barely sleep at all. In the morning, we begin the routine again, but this time, our numbers have somehow grown.

Finally, late in the afternoon, we enter Carabas land. I lean out the window, trying to get a glimpse of the castle ahead of us. Instead, my eyes stray to the farmers working the early spring fields.

"Who does this land belong to?" the king calls out.

A nearby farmer and his wife look up, smiles on their faces. "The Marquis of Carabas, My Lord."

I suck in a gasp and nearly throw myself out of the moving carriage. The king, Kerrick, and Sabine all holler at me to come back, but I run toward the couple.

The pair gawks at me, their eyes drifting to the hem of my gown, which is now coated with mud.

"What has happened to Lord Mattis?" I demand.

"The curse has been lifted—the ogre is dead," the man says. "The Marquis has returned."

Squealing in the most unladylike sort of way, I rush back to the carriage. The nobles stare at me, surprised.

"Hurry," I urge, ignoring the footman's outstretched hand as I leap up the stairs. "He's done it. Beau's killed the ogre!"

The king and Kerrick look unsure, but Sabine is taken in with my enthusiasm, and she beams at me. Her little dog jumps from the princess's lap onto mine and then back again, yapping.

We slow as we grow near the drawbridge, but a guard calls down to us, "You are very welcome, Your Majesty. The marquis is expecting you."

I'm the first out of the carriage, and I scan the courtyard, searching for Beau. I don't look long. He's standing at the entrance, his arms behind his back, a solemn look on his face.

But when he sees me, his eyes brighten and he runs forward, catching me in his arms. Laughing, I hold him tight.

"How did you do it?" I ask, burying my face in the crook of his neck.

"It was Puss." He pulls me back, studying my face as if he's drinking me in.

As I stand here, astonished, Beau tells me how the ogre met his end.

I look around the courtyard. "Where are all the dwarves?" The trees are quiet as well. "And the fairies."

Beau's expression softens. "Most are gone, though a few linger. They are free."

"As are you," I murmur.

Just as he's about to speak, we're interrupted by the others. Beau releases me and bows to the king.

"I hear you've rid yourself of an ogre," His Majesty says, grinning. "It seems we have traveled all this way for nothing."

"Not for nothing, Your Majesty," Beau says. He turns to me, his expression hopeful but his eyes betraying his nervousness. "You once said you wanted to see the home of the *Marquise* of Carabas."

My heart stutters. "What are you saying?"

Beau smiles, hopeful. "Marry me, Etta."

Agreeing, I leap into his arms.

"Enough of this," Puss says, taking more than a few people by surprise. "A feast has been prepared in the king's honor. Let's not let it grow cold."

CHAPTER 47

Etta

THE SEA STRETCHES OUT IN FRONT OF US, FULL OF INFINITE opportunities. I lean on the railing, taking it in. Behind me, Beau and Thomas argue about which island we should visit next.

We met with Thomas at a port city near the coast, and my brother agreed to travel with us for a time. So far we've bought chocolate, spices, and coffee, and I've seen places I've never dreamed of.

Beau says we'll return home in a few months, back to the Carabas estate. Eugene and Sarah-Anne live there now, away from Monsieur Broussard and the mill that's full of sad memories. Eugene has stepped into the role of Beau's steward, and the position fits my brother well.

Beau's ship rocks with the waves, and it seems eager to be away from the dock.

"You look very serious." Beau kisses my shoulder and wraps his arms around my waist.

I glance back at my new husband. "Only happy."

He hands me a paper-wrapped package. "A runner has just brought your purchase. Can we leave now?"

Peeling back the paper, I take a peek in the parcel and smile. Standing on my toes, I press a soft kiss to Beau's lips.

"Now we can."

I leave Beau on the deck and make my way to the captain's cabin, where Puss has taken up residence. I find him stretched out in the middle of the bed, cuddled into the silken cover. A half-drank bowl of cream sits on the table, but the plate holding his fish breakfast has been licked clean.

"I have something for you," I say as I sit next to him.

He peeks his eyes open, trying to decide if my gift is worth waking up for. I set the package in front of him and slowly pull back the paper, revealing a tiny pair of boots. Curious, now awake, Puss sniffs the gift and then turns his attention toward me. "Boots?"

"And a tiny hat." I hold it up for him to inspect. "Complete with a little feather."

Puss looks at the gifts uncertainly. "You shouldn't have."

Grinning, I slide the boots on his feet and secure the hat to his head. "What do you think?"

The cat stands, frozen, on the bed. And then, quite suddenly, he falls over, stiff as a board.

"What's the matter?" I ask, laughing. "Don't you like them?"

He begins kicking his feet, trying to work the boots off. "I think I'll leave wearing the boots to you."

Taking pity on him, I pull the hat from his head as well and cuddle him on my lap. Looking around the ornate captain's cabin, I stroke under his chin like he likes. "What do you think, Puss. Is it grand enough?"

From above, I hear the calls of the crew as the ship leaves the dock.

"Yes, Etta." The cat rubs against my hand, purring, and then collapses on his pillows. "I think we did very well indeed."

THE QUEEN OF GOLD AND STRAW

Available November 19, 2018

Click Here to View the Book on Amazon

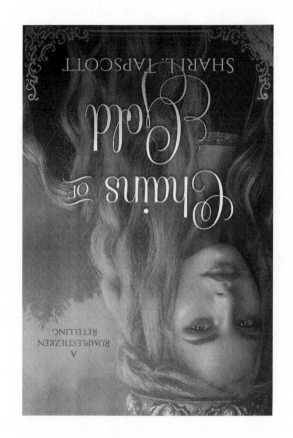

A
RUMPLESTILTZKEN
RETELLING

Chains of Gold

SHARI L. TAPSCOTT

ABOUT THE AUTHOR

Shari L. Tapscott writes young adult fantasy and humorous contemporary fiction. When she's not writing or reading, she enjoys gardening, making soap, and pretending she can sing. She loves white chocolate mochas, furry animals, spending time with her family, and characters who refuse to behave.

Tapscott lives in western Colorado with her husband, son, daughter, and two very spoiled Saint Bernards.

sharitapscott.com